VAPOR

By the Author

I Dare You

No Leavin' Love

The Pleasure Planner

Vapor

VAPOR

by
Larkin Rose

2010

VAPOR

ISBN 10:1-60282-155-0
ISBN 13:978-1-60282-155-2

This Trade Paperback Original Is Published By
Bold Strokes Books, Inc.
P.O. Box 249
Valley Falls, NY 12185

First Edition: June 2010

CREDITS
EDITOR: CINDY CRESAP
PRODUCTION DESIGN: STACIA SEAMAN
COVER DESIGN BY SHERI (GRAPHICARTIST2020@HOTMAIL.COM)

Acknowledgments

To Cindy: Has anyone told you lately that you ROCK?

To Rad: The BSB family is incredible. I'm such a lucky girl to be part of it. Thank you!

Dedication

To the readers: as always, every word, sentence,
and paragraph is for you and only you.

Dalia…I still don't know what I'd do without you.
You're stuck with me!

To Rose…14 years and counting.
I wouldn't change a single second.

CHAPTER ONE

"I want to smell you." Michelle froze when Andrea took a deliberate step toward her, the strobe lights from the nightclub arcing across her face, making her jade eyes blaze with desire. Corded muscles jerked to attention along her upper arm as she reached for Michelle. Her shoulders bunched inside her sleeveless T-shirt, her normal weekend attire that only added delicious flavor to her loose-fitting jeans. "I want to taste you, to feel you pump around my tongue."

Ashley Vaughn took a casual glance around the small bookstore, sizing up the crowd's reaction to the reading. Had she gone too far with her description, with her non–purple prose dialogue? Would this small-town audience appreciate the difficult choice she'd made to step outside the romance box and into the world of erotic writing?

By the smiles on a few faces, they didn't seem offended by such directness. Would they be totally offended if they knew she was imagining each and every one of them naked in their chairs? Would they be disgusted to know she also imagined them bald and wearing bright red clown noses? It seemed to be the only way she could gather the courage to stand before them to read the short story from the anthology. The excitement of having one of her stories accepted by a publisher hadn't diminished in the months from acceptance to publication. It wasn't what she'd always dreamed of, having a single title with her name on the cover, and it wasn't New York, but it was a start.

When no one shoved out of their chairs or raced for the exit, she glanced back down at the page she was reading.

Michelle swallowed back a moan, fearful Andrea would hear the quiver in the sound and know she was weak with need...that Andrea was making her weak with desire.

Weak, she was...weak...for this woman. The very woman who seemed to rob her of common sense every time she was near her. Every Friday and Saturday night, to be exact, she came to this club with her friends, specifically to ogle the sexy bartender, to watch her woo and tease her customers into some ridiculous version of Adults Gone Wild. *And now, here she was, all but jacked against the wall, with Andrea's jade eyes narrowed into slits, seducing her with erotic words, just like she'd watched her do to so many other women on so many other nights. She'd fantasized about this very encounter, what she'd do to Andrea, what Andrea would do to her. And now she was going to find out.*

Apprehension took over. This wasn't like her. Andrea was definitely behaving like herself, but Michelle was far from it. She wasn't looking for casual sex. She could find that in every bar along the West Coast. What she was looking for, Andrea couldn't provide. Love.

She opened her mouth to protest but Andrea's finger silenced her. "Don't, Michelle. Don't. I've waited long enough."

Andrea's husky whisper sent hot prickles searing across her pussy. Had she heard Andrea right? Did she want her? Michelle almost snorted at her own brainless question. Of course Andrea wanted her. She wasn't a notch on her bedpost yet. Andrea was after the kill...one more fuck to brag to her buddies about.

Ashley looked up from the page. Eager faces watched her, waiting for the sexual scene to unfold. She'd just used the p-word and not a single person had gasped, or scoffed, or barged from the room.

She found her spot on the page and continued.

The breath whooshed from her lungs when Andrea crushed their bodies together, her tongue breaking the barrier to force inside Michelle's mouth.

She expelled a groan and wove her fingers into Andrea's hair, pulling her closer, thrusting greedily against her. How could she want this woman so bad? How could she possibly need sex from somebody who used women then tossed them aside like a discarded Sunday newspaper?

Because she knew the sex would be mind-blowing, that's why. If only once, she wanted to discover what Andrea Walker had that other women didn't and maybe experience the perfect fuck. She had no illusions. Andrea would forget her before the night was over. So what? The toe-curling, back-arching, subliminal sex would be worth every flick of those slender fingers and every swipe of the tongue swirling inside her mouth.

Ashley looked out over the crowd once again. Half the room was on the edge of their seats, anticipating, almost demanding her to continue.

Happiness spread through her and her limbs tingled. A flush heated her cheeks. They truly liked what she was reading. Their pleasure was written all over their hopeful faces as they hung on her every word, like little children gazing longingly at their favorite treat.

When her gaze landed on dark eyes in the back of the room, Ashley felt warmth spread down her neck. Liquid heat pooled against her thong as the woman crossed her arms and stared back, her sights trickling down Ashley's body before coming to rest on her face again. In the dimness of the corner, Ashley couldn't make out her features, but those penetrating eyes were unmistakably measuring every inch of her.

Ashley took a deep breath and started reading again, not from the pages this time, but from memory.

Andrea pumped against her, hard, almost lifting Michelle off her feet with sweet brutality.

She wrapped one leg around Andrea's waist and met those demanding drives, fiercely grasping thick handfuls of hair, raking nails down her back, clinging to Andrea like it would be the last time she ever could...the last time she knew she ever would.

Ashley never broke the silent connection with the sexy stranger. She read to her, for her, and only her. Suddenly, no one else existed in the room. The bald, naked people with their red radiant noses were gone. Just the two of them: one seducing with words, the other with her eyes, but it was seduction nonetheless.

When Andrea grabbed the cheeks of her ass and hoisted her up around her waist, Michelle lost herself in the moment. She no longer cared that Andrea wouldn't remember this night, no longer cared that she herself would never forget.

Tonight, if only for tonight, she was going to drown in these minutes, then hold them close to her heart forever. All the nights, all the months of watching her, wanting her, needing her...in seconds the lust would be over, and so would all the wishful thinking that someone like Andrea Walker could want someone like Michelle Bradford.

Michelle held on tight as Andrea stumbled down the alcove leading to the back room, her mouth still sealed, that glorious tongue still rounding inside her mouth. She tasted so good, unlike Michelle assumed she'd taste.

Instead of whiskey, she tasted of fruity gum. And her hair was so silky it practically dripped through her fingers every time she fisted her hand.

When they crashed through a door, Michelle tightened her legs around her hips, now palming her cheeks, fearing Andrea would break the contact.

Within minutes, their sex would be over. Within hours, Michelle would be lost.

She knew she'd never walk back into this bar again. She couldn't. She wouldn't watch the love of her life pawing at another, teasing, and then walking out that door at the end of the night arm in arm. It'd break her in half, she knew. The one woman she'd secretly wanted for far too long was out of reach. But tonight, she was all hers.

With a grunt, she pushed all thoughts to the back of her mind. Right now, she was too far gone to turn back the hands of time. She would finish this, and she would remember every delicious detail for the rest of her life.

Andrea dropped Michelle onto a desk, broke the seal of their kiss, then with a brush of her arm, swiped all of the contents onto the floor. Papers fluttered through the air like overgrown butterflies before landing softly on the carpet. A cup of pens landed with a clatter and scattered in all directions.

Andrea wrapped her hand around the back of Michelle's neck and pulled her into another heated kiss, this time not so harsh...this time slow, and casual, and fuck almighty, so sexy.

She licked Michelle's bottom lip, then sucked it between her teeth before she snaked her tongue back into Michelle's mouth.

Michelle expelled a moan, her insides knotting, her pussy pulsing, and her mind numb. This was going to be the most glorious experience of her life, and yet, the most gut wrenching.

Why couldn't she just tell Andrea how she felt? Why

was it so hard to declare her feelings? Was it easier to just fuck and walk away, always looking for the next sexual fling?

When Andrea wedged between her thighs, Michelle told herself she didn't care, that she couldn't change Andrea. Andrea didn't want to be changed.

Andrea pulled away and knelt, kissing a trail inside her knees just beneath the edge of her skirt. "Tell me how you like it, Michelle."

Michelle couldn't admit she liked it slow, lasting, and cuddling when it was all over. What a laugh Andrea would get out of that confession.

"I like it hard, baby. As hard as you can give it to me," Michelle lied.

Andrea smiled and shoved her legs apart.

Michelle gasped, her pussy aflame with the need for Andrea to take her, to make her come harder than she would probably ever come again in her life.

Michelle sighed in heated pleasure as Andrea slid her hands up her inner thighs, pushing the thin material up. With those green eyes watching her, Andrea knotted her fingers into the strings on either side of her thigh, and then slowly tugged her thong down and off.

She pulled Michelle to the edge of the desk, opened her legs wider, exposing Michelle to her sights, then began those glorious fiery kisses again.

"Why do you come to this bar, Michelle?" Andrea dragged her tongue along her flesh then nipped.

Michelle groaned and let her head fall back. "The music. And my friends."

"That's all?" Andrea gave the same torture to the opposite leg.

Michelle ground her teeth against the intensity, circling her hips toward Andrea, desperate for her hot mouth to clamp around her clit. "Maybe not."

Andrea pressed her tongue along her slit and Michelle froze in anticipation.

When Andrea's warm breath feathered against her clit, Michelle knew she would come undone before Andrea latched onto her. Her insides were on fire and fuck if it didn't feel good.

"I watch you," Andrea whispered.

What? *Michelle pulled her head forward to look down at Andrea. She didn't learn anything in Andrea's expression and her eyes were closed, her mouth still busy working kisses along her skin. Had she heard her right?* Andrea watched her? Why?

Duh. Of course she did. How else could she know that she needed to add to her little black book?

"I watch you, too, sexy. Everyone in this bar does, as you well know."

"Everyone else doesn't matter." Andrea reversed her path until she hit the center spot. The tip of her tongue tagged the very tip of Michelle's hood and she practically jerked right off the desk.

Andrea wedged her back in place with strong hands and flicked her tongue once again.

Michelle tossed her head back, wanting desperately to continue their conversation...to even fucking remember what they were talking about.

Watching her...no one else mattered. That was it!

What the fuck did that mean? Were these sweet nothings the same things she told every one of her fucks? Of course it was. She was a player.

Michelle gathered her thoughts in the few seconds between flicks of that soft tongue. "You're right. No one else matters right now but me. It's my turn for that notch on your bedpost." She circled her hips for another lashing, but got nothing.

She opened her eyes and looked down, and found

those green eyes staring back at her, a hard expression taking over Andrea's otherwise gorgeous face.

When Andrea stood, Michelle wanted to shove her back down on her knees, wanted to clench her legs around her face and thrash against her. Fuck, she needed to come so bad it was torturous.

"A notch on my bedpost? What the hell does that mean?"

Michelle saw hurt nestled in those eyes. The expression confused her. Andrea didn't strike her as a person to get her feelings hurt. Hell, she wasn't sure a woman like Andrea even had feelings.

"It's okay, sexy. I don't care." Damn it, she was lying again. She did care. So why was she here in the back room, her legs spread wide before Andrea Walker, the sexiest woman collector she'd ever known?

The answer was sick. Because she was in love with her, and if this was the only part of Andrea she could have, she was going to take it. That simple.

"Is that what you think this is?" Andrea drew back, anger firing rapidly in her eyes.

Michelle resisted reaching for her by shoving her skirt back into place. "Isn't it?"

"No, Michelle, it isn't." Andrea forked her fingers through her hair and looked at the floor. "I...feel things."

Michelle cocked her head to the side. Andrea seemed alien-like at this moment. She wasn't sure how to react, or if she should at all. Was this part of the player's game?

She didn't know enough about Andrea to know that answer. But Christ if she didn't look genuine. And sad.

"Feel...things?" Michelle shifted uncomfortably on the desk, her insides coiled tight as a jack-in-the-box. "I don't understand."

In a blink of an eye, Andrea grabbed her wrist and tugged her off the desk. "I feel things, Michelle..." She hung her head for a second. "When you're here, with your friends, dancing with other women, laughing with them, sometimes kissing them. I feel things that I don't understand."

Michelle was dumbfounded. Was this some sick, and sweet, way of Andrea declaring her feelings?

Fuck almighty but the thought was too incredible.

Women like Andrea didn't love women like Michelle. Well, maybe in the movies, but not out here in the real world where blond bombshells with IQs the size of slugs and tits the size of watermelons ruled the nightclub scenes.

Michelle wasn't like those women; though she'd always wished she was...it might have scored her a night with Andrea much sooner. By now, she'd already be over the damage.

But the look on Andrea's face made her want to curl into her arms. If she was playing a game, she was doing a damn good job at it.

Michelle lifted Andrea's chin with the tip of her finger. She had to see those eyes. The truth would be there, she was sure. The eyes could never lie.

And what she found made her stumble back against the desk. "Andrea, what are you saying?"

Andrea followed, pinning Michelle between those tight thighs and the hard desk. "I'm saying I want something more than..." She waved her hand in the air. "...a fuck. I want to take you to dinner, or to a movie. I want to snuggle on a couch, under a blanket, and watch a movie that makes you cry...so I can wipe away your tears."

When Michelle cocked her brow, frozen in shocked silence, Andrea snickered. "Sounds corny, huh?"

Good Lord, Andrea Walker had just declared her feelings for the underdog.

Michelle caught each side of her face and pulled her forward.

"Coming from you, hell yes, that's corny." She kissed

the tip of her nose. "And it's the most beautiful thing I've ever heard."

Andrea nuzzled her neck. "Can we get out of here?"

"I thought you'd never ask."

When the crowd broke into applause, Ashley blinked and looked down at the book in her hand, at the page marked with her thumb. According to the page number, she still had a page and half to read. Had she just read the entire short story without ever flipping the page...without taking her sights off the mysterious stranger?

By the reaction unfolding in front of her, women clapping wildly, some catcalling, cheering, and whistling, she was positive she had.

Her heart swelled as couples gathered around her, thrusting the anthology into her hands. She gave her best smile and let her gaze roam the room. The woman still leaned against the wall, those muscular arms still folded, and those smoldering dark eyes still watching.

Ashley dropped into the chair behind the card table and began signing her first autographs. She knew she'd never forget this day, even if her writing adventures never took her beyond the yearly print anthologies...even if her work never made it to New York's door.

These women appreciated her work, and that meant more than any New York contract ever could. *Yeah, right.* Who the hell was she kidding? She wanted to write for New York like she needed Hardee's to bring back the Chili Cheese Thickburger. It was her goal, her lifelong dream, and even if they continued to snub their noses, she'd keep poking her manuscripts in their faces.

Book after book, she scribbled her name onto the blank front pages, while wondering why the sexy stranger hadn't come forward. A quick glance showed the woman had moved her location, now holding a copy of the anthology, but still lagging at the back of the crowd.

Would she come forward? Obviously, she planned to. She'd waited this long, right? Could Ashley stand it if she didn't?

The slick mess between her thighs proved she couldn't.

"I must say, I'm enthralled with your work." A femme with a wide smile and long brown hair handed Ashley the book.

Ashley returned the smile. "Thank you for saying so. I was a little worried how the crowd would react to the bold scenes."

"I wish more authors weren't afraid to venture outside the box. We readers want to see beyond that closed door."

Ashley appreciated her words…and lived them daily. She, too, was sick of living inside that box. Of course, she had to admit, she'd grown up with the straight conventional romance novels, where the hero rescued the heroine from some mortal danger, and they both lived happily ever after.

Christ on a stick, there were only so many of those damn things a girl could read. Where was the sex? Why did the author find the need to slam that door in the reader's face when the heat was boiling both characters to unbearable temperatures? Why, oh why, couldn't they see what happened after the pawing began?

And fuck, why in the hell didn't the authors credit the reader with some intelligence and allow them to see the main characters ripping at each other, too consumed by the moment to wait another second, when the desires and needs were too far gone to seek privacy? Wasn't that real life?

That's what Ashley wanted, that's what she gave her readers, but until now, she hadn't known how they would accept her love for living beyond that bedroom door. It gave her another rush to know she'd touched these people, and might be touching thousands more.

So, if it was so easy for this woman to admit she'd found a thrill in Ashley's reading, why was it so damn hard for New York? Was it her style, or her voice?

With a shrug, she waved off the thoughts. Time. Time would help her reach her goal. And maybe some begging. Begging could help. Maybe.

When another woman approached and held out the book, Ashley took a quick glance down the line and was overwhelmed with a flush of heat when she saw there were only a few people remaining, one of them being the mystery woman who'd made her feel like a horny teenager once again.

The lights fell around her, showing off short dark hair highlighted by Ms. Clairol and a chunking cap. The woman lifted her gaze from the book in her hand and eyes the color of chocolate mousse met Ashley's. She reeled, as she had from the impact of that damn dodge ball back in elementary school, the one that knocked her flat on her ass while all the little boys pointed and laughed, and Sarah Littlejohn oohed in amazement at the way Ashley was still coherent after such a blow.

She almost tilted out of the chair under the woman's scrutiny, and her pussy clenched with sweet pain. She couldn't remember ever being affected like this by a stranger, and memorized the feeling for later use in one of her novels—and a detailed description of those eyes—if she dared ever write another one, that is. The first, and only, novel was collecting a few inches of dust particles on her hard drive.

As quickly as she could, Ashley signed the next book, then another, and when she slowly looked up, knowing her stranger was going to be standing over her all barbarian-like, she found a couple giving her a sickeningly sweet smile, as if Ashley held all the answers.

She looked around the couple, and found the last customers in line and her mystery woman at the very end.

What the fuck was she doing? Teasing? Hell, it was working. Ashley was a wet mess from the mere anticipation of her approach.

She all but yanked the book from the couple, asked their names, and scribbled something she hoped would be readable later, then handed it back.

The next, and thank God, the last, and suddenly she was looking up into those dreamy eyes. *Heaven.* That's where this woman had come from. Only God could make a woman so perfect...chiseled nose swiped right off the face of a statue, high cheekbones, perfect shaped lips, and the faint edging of a smile. Crooked. Her smile was crooked. And dear God, a single dimple on her left cheek. *Kill me now!* It made her all the sexier and Ashley wanted to rise from her chair, crawl across the flimsy table like a lioness, and lick the natural sheen right off of her lips.

With the suave mannerism she could have only been born with, because Lord knew one couldn't acquire that kind of haughty sex appeal any other way, the woman held out her book.

Ashley stared at long, tapering fingers, well imagining how tight they'd fit in her pussy, how bad she wanted to ride them until she creamed all over them.

With as much composure as she could gather, she let her gaze climb sporty thighs wrapped loosely in a pair of stonewashed jeans, along a tight stomach encased in a peach-colored Izod shirt, then along her throat, until she met those eyes.

Fuck…she was going to drown in those eyes.

CHAPTER TWO

Victoria Hadley moved closer until she towered over the sexy author, beside herself with hunger, desire, and splendidly wet from the reading. She followed a long, raven black curl over Ashley's shoulder, watched it round beneath one breast like a lover's hand. She imagined her own palm replacing the lock of hair, and her pussy clenched with need. The woman was more breathtaking in the flesh than in the picture on her Web site. Definitely sexier. The lone image of her resting against oversized pillows, a mischievous grin playing along her lips, showed a playful side of her. The real woman sitting before her was far from playful. Right now she was sex on a stick and flirty as hell. And Vic wanted, needed, to satisfy the incredible hunger that Ashley had stirred in her gut.

The way Ashley had made eye contact then spoken every word while staring her down, as if she'd written the entire story especially for Vic alone, had been excruciating. She'd been frozen in place as Ashley's seductive voice crept into her very soul and then bore it away to some magical place where anything was possible.

Had Vic known a book signing would have slicked her pussy this way, she would have attended every erotic reading available within a hundred-mile radius of Arizona.

No! Who was she kidding? She almost chuckled at the insinuation. Attending any other reading wouldn't have done her a bit of good. There wasn't another damn author alive who could have serenaded her with words the way Ashley Vaughn had just done.

Those lips. Vic had been hypnotized from the second she'd parted them, completely sucked into the tantalizing details rolling off their plumpness. Seductive and dripping with sex, those lips were so perfect they could have been stenciled from the very hands of Leonardo da Vinci. Perfect for kissing. Vic had thought of nothing else from the second Ashley had trapped her in that hypnotic gaze. From the back of the room, even with the light filtering down to highlight Ashley in her high-powered business suit of dark brown slacks and creamy-colored blouse, she couldn't tell what color her eyes were. Now she knew they were amber, and beautiful, and watching her.

"Hi." Vic wanted to say more, but her mind suddenly went blank, the details from the reading still playing like an erotic video inside her head, with Vic and Ashley in the roles of Andrea and Michelle. Experiencing the exquisite torture of their coming together, yet not coming, that was the greatest torture of all.

Ashley had pitched her story like a pro, though Vic knew this was her very first reading. She'd been following this newbie author since her fuck buddy, Heather, had introduced her to the anthology a few months earlier. Reading wasn't much of a hobby as she found most books rather boring. She quickly tired of authors who slammed the door in her face as soon as the characters approached the bedroom.

But not Ashley. Oh no. She'd given Vic exactly what she'd wanted. A believable story about real people. Hot sex, tantalizing description of the foreplay without any prudish euphemisms or lack of detail, and plenty of erotic passages to get the juices flowing.

However, she'd been bummed to find out the author didn't have other titles on the market. The story in the one anthology was all she had published, which was surprising since Vic had read nothing but shit from the tiny lesbian section tucked into the farthest corner of the bookstore. She liked to think of that darkened area as the "naughty" corner, though until now, naughty hadn't exactly been offered, which is why reading was for boring, rainy days only, and until now, rarely spiked her sex drive.

And now, she was standing before the woman who had turned

her crotch into a fire pit, staring down at her, lost for words, her mind packed with all the delicious ways she could fuck her and keep on doing so until they were both sated.

Can you sign my book and put out the fire you started...with your mouth? Oh, if only she could say those words aloud, but of course, she couldn't. Hysterical laughter bubbled in Vic's throat just picturing the scene if she dared such a bold move. The bookstore owner would probably kick her out and maybe ban her for life. Or even worse, Ashley would scoff and label her a stalker.

But she had dared, in her mind. In her mind's eye, she'd just fucked Ashley on that damn desk right after she raked the contents onto the floor. She'd nibbled her inner thighs just as Andrea had done to Michelle, kissed and licked her way up those lean legs, though she hadn't stopped. Oh no, she couldn't have stopped. In her wild imagination, Ashley had screamed and come so hard around Vic's tongue. She'd whimpered like a newborn pup and thrashed against Vic's face like a shock victim while she cried out her name over and over and over. Vic shuddered and clamped her thighs together to trap the hot talons tearing at her crotch. What she wouldn't give to feel those spasms in real life.

Yet, she didn't know why. What made Ashley Vaughn so special? She'd had other women. Not many, but enough. None had ever exerted such a pull over her. Not one had dominated her from across the room with a teasing, seductive stare and a mouthful of sexy words streaming one after the other.

Was that it? Had Ashley entranced and captivated her with nothing more than paper scenery? Was the attraction she felt merely the result of Ashley reciting words from a page, giving her the sex behind the closed doors she truly wanted to read, and hear? She frowned and focused on Ashley's face, looking for confirmation.

Ashley's brow cocked and a smile teetered. "Did you want me to guess who I should sign this to?"

Vic cleared her throat, embarrassed that Ashley had caught her daydreaming about sex. And not just sex per se but also indulging in a wild, unconventional sexual fantasy based on the reading. What a lush she must look like. She stood a little taller. "No one."

"No one?" That smile deepened on those kissable mocha-colored lips. "Does *no one* have a first or last name?"

Vic stammered. "No, I mean...that's not my..." She drew in an unsteady breath, heat crawling in a fine line along her neck and cheeks. *Christ.* She was blushing in front of Ashley Vaughn, for God's sake. She never blushed. It was so wimpy, and so not for butches. Seriously, this was not the first impression she wanted to imprint on this beauty. "Vic, my name is Vic. And I don't want your autograph...just yet."

When Ashley arched her brow, questioning the hiatus, Vic inhaled again, this time catching a sweet scent that could only belong to the goddess sitting in front of her. The delightful floral aroma calmed her, allowing her brain to function.

"Hello, Vic. And when, exactly, did you want my autograph?"

Oh man, just hearing her name roll off those plump lips made her want to drop like a football player for a hike, crawl beneath the table, and slam Ashley's legs apart. Sweet pain seared her crotch as she controlled the impulse.

"Have you eaten? I'm starving." Vic let her gaze slide down Ashley's neck to her breasts where prominent nipples pressed against the thin silky material of her top, then lower across a flat stomach, only stopping when the table wouldn't allow her to look farther. Jeez! Ashley looked good enough to eat, like creamy vanilla ice cream with a luscious raspberry topping. Vic sighed longingly. She'd certainly delight in licking every last inch of that delectable body and then come back for more.

When Vic looked back into those gorgeous amber eyes, she saw amusement. What was Ashley thinking? Could she read Vic's mind from her expression alone? Did she wonder if Vic might be a dangerous psychopath? Hell, who would blame her any such thoughts? She sure hadn't given Ashley any reason to be impressed with her so far. She needed to pull herself together and demonstrate to Ms. Sexy Vaughn what set her apart and made her special, or at least different from all the other women who'd clustered around her this afternoon. Except that wasn't so easy to do.

Not only was Vic confused by her reaction to Ashley and this situation, she was also confused about her actions. Never had a woman made her stutter like an unbalanced idiot before. The fact that Ashley had drawn out this new behavior made her question the reason. She needed to know why she was behaving like a lovesick teen instead of a mature thirty-four-year-old who happened to own her own five-star restaurant.

Was it her looks? No. She'd had many women just as beautiful and just as sexy as Ashley. Okay, so maybe not quite as gorgeous, and maybe not nearly as sexy, but close enough. It wasn't as if she was butt-ugly and had to make do with the second-rate women nobody else wanted.

She had pride. Right now, that pride was oozing out all over the damn place.

"No, actually, I haven't eaten." Ashley teased with a slow glide of those eyes down Vic's body, stalling on the vee between her legs. Her tongue snaked out to circle her lips, leaving behind an enticing film of moisture. "And I'm starving, too."

Vic could almost feel that tongue teasing her clit into a long, drawn-out, screaming orgasm. She controlled the urge to clench her legs together to ease the throbbing ache caused by Ashley's words and forced herself to meet that taunting stare with a degree of equanimity that belied the turmoil twisting her stomach into knots. "Then may I extend an invitation for dinner? My treat."

Dammit, she sounded like some Victorian maiden, all prim and proper. What the fuck was she doing? And why was she doing it? Silly question. She wanted to wine and dine Ashley then take her to bed and feast on her delectable body for the rest of the night.

"Yes, you may."

Vic blinked at the ready acceptance. Either Ashley was desperate, or she was totally enthralled by the unusual nature of this invitation, and where it might lead them, to turn her down.

Either way, she didn't care. Ashley Vaughn had just accepted a dinner date, desperate or not.

"And where will you be, um, treating me?" The smile on her

lips moved to her eyes and Vic couldn't look away from the attractive feather-like laughter lines across her temple. *On this carpet, or right here on this fucking table.*

Vic swallowed hard, hastily shoving back the images of a naked Ashley draped over the table for her pleasure, with her thighs spread wide, of her screaming as she pumped against her mouth or hand, her insides throbbing with an orgasm.

"Ellirondos."

Ashley narrowed her eyes. "*You wish.* From what I've heard the menu there is so good that no one gets a reservation less than a month in advance."

Pride swelled Vic's ego that Ashley would know that bit of information about her restaurant.

Lucky for Ashley, Vic happened to own the place, a fact she'd keep to herself for the time being. If her night with the sexy author proved fatal, at least she wouldn't have blown her cover.

With a smile, Vic took the unsigned book from her grasp. "Then I get to impress you by getting us in on short notice. And then I'll take that autograph."

"You're on." Ashley shook her head and laughed. "This I've got to see."

"Make it seven. I'll be waiting." Vic forced herself to walk away, knowing Ashley's gaze was eating her alive with every step.

If the stars were with her, tonight she'd be eating Ashley Vaughn alive.

Chapter Three

A shley pulled her aging Celica against the curb and took an unsteady breath. She'd fought with several outfits, finally compromising on a thin chiffon skirt short enough to show off her newly shaped legs thanks to *Thighs and Buns of Steel*. God only knew why, as she hated the damn things. Easy access? Without a doubt, she knew that was the reason. Only the possibility of sex would make her wear anything less than jeans outside of work.

She glanced at the silk blouse, and after several mental arguments with herself, she plucked open the button to show a little more cleavage.

Her heart beat a little faster as the decisive moment approached. The prospect of this dinner date intrigued her beyond anything she'd experienced in a long time, and from such a sexy invitation, how could she refuse? Until now, she'd only admired the five-star restaurant from the cobblestone sidewalk while on a lazy evening stroll after dining at some lesser place. Tonight she'd be entering its lair, provided Vic had pulled off the impossible and secured a table.

Light streamed from every window and from the large brass sconces on either side of the entrance making the building a beacon of light against the otherwise drab night sky. Groups of people lined the ivy-clad walls patiently waiting outside the restaurant in vain hope of securing a cancellation. Beyond the window, the brightly lit dining room showcased elegance at its finest. She couldn't wait to step inside for the first time. God knew it'd probably be her last since this Italian steakhouse charged the earth and it almost took the death of a patron to open up a spot on the reservation list.

The valet had the door open before she could even reach for the handle, his hand outstretched to assist her from the car. He waved away her tip and nodded toward the sidewalk.

There stood her butch in shining armor, black slacks encasing long, lean legs. Her heart stumbled as Vic gave her a lethal smile. Ashley reminded herself she was thirty-one with pride and self-control, not eighteen and loose as a goose. Neither wining nor dining could get into her pants, right? Well, maybe. The way Vic looked right now, anything was possible—food or no food. And who was she kidding? She'd worn this outfit with every intention of fucking Vic.

Ashley licked her lips as she stepped to the curb on wobbly knees. She mentally cursed her choice of high heels. Had she known the sight of this hunk of burning lust would turn her into slush, she'd have worn flats, though either choice wouldn't stop the quiver snaking through her body. She took in Vic's pale gray button-up shirt. Damn, if she didn't clean up well after trading in her denim jeans and golf attire. Though she had to admit the Levi's had fit her curves deliciously, a fact she vowed to share with her sexy date at some point during her dinner, though showing her was way up top of her priority list.

"You look stunning." Vic took her hand, pulled her closer, and then placed a delicate kiss on her cheek. "So glad you didn't change your mind."

Ashley gave her a quizzical stare. "How could I pass up an invitation to one of the hottest spots in Phoenix? Do you know how many prayers go out daily for people to get hit by a Mack truck so they'll move up faster on the reservation list?" She gave a scornful stare. "Do you own a Mack truck, by chance?"

Vic laughed and Ashley could feel the seams of her soul splitting apart. Holy hell, what was it? Her looks, her suave manners? Something, dadgumit, was making her act like a giddy thirteen-year-old. "Guess that gives new meaning to the old saying 'the food is to die for,' huh? And no, I didn't murder anyone to snag us a table."

Ashley willed her gaze away from those trance-inducing eyes to glance through the window. A waiter angled a bottle of wine in front of his customers, a white linen napkin draped over his arm. He was posture perfect as he tilted the bottle over their wineglasses.

"Shall we go inside?" Vic placed a firm hand against the small of her back and Ashley obediently moved forward.

She frowned when the host did a double take as Vic strode up to her station and announced, "I have a table reserved in the back."

In the back? Ashley almost choked, cursing herself for the heat crawling across her cheeks. Of course their table would be in the back. And fuck almighty, where the hell were all these blushes coming from? She didn't blush, ever. So what was with this heat spiraling down the sides of her neck? And where was it coming from?

The host gave Ashley careful scrutiny, and then turned back to Vic, a smile threatening her lips as if she knew a secret and liked knowing it all by her little lonesome. "Of course. Follow me, please." She picked up two menus and escorted them to a table tucked into a dimly lit corner. ·

Was her date somebody famous? Ashley's heart flipped at this incredible thought. She certainly behaved as if she were a celebrity who had no need to give her name. And the host appeared to accept her right not to do so.

Vic waited for Ashley to sit before she slid into the chair next to her. A candle flickered inside a crystal vase, casting a dull shadow against Vic's face.

Man, oh man, but she was gorgeous in about every butch way possible. Her dark eyes bore no secret that dinner—and this evening—might last deep into the morning hours. Ashley said a silent prayer that she'd be kissing the morning sun with a scream pouring from her lips, very much like her characters played out on the pages of her computer.

Could it be possible for her to live some of their realities tonight?

A waitress was beside the table in a flash to take their order, her hair neatly combed back away from her youthful face into a long single braid down her back, and a bottle of wine lying delicately in her hands. "May I offer..." She narrowed her eyes when she looked at Vic. "Um, a glass of Cuvee Imperiale?"

Ashley watched the interaction, wondering if Vic had this kind of effect on every woman she came in contact with, young or old. The woman was like a walking sex magnet, so what was she doing sitting here in such a fine restaurant with such a dull recluse like Ashley?

It gave Ashley a boost to think of herself as the mystery woman. Vic didn't know anything about her, only that she was an author, and that she'd read hot sex for a room full of lesbians. For all she knew, Ashley could be a best-selling author who traveled near and far like a movie star.

Phfft. Who was she kidding? No one would ever think that about her, and if New York didn't hurry and get their nose out of their ass, she'd never see any scenery outside of the boring desert of Arizona.

"Yes, and we'll take a bottle of Amarone della Valpolicella." Vic eyed Ashley for her approval.

Ashley snapped back a gasp. Dinner on short notice at a place almost impossible to obtain a reservation, and now some nifty-priced wine that sounded damn sexy rolling off Vic's tongue. Oh yeah, someone was going to get fucked tonight, and from the deadly smile Vic was passing across the table, Ashley was positive it was going to be her.

She nodded and smoothed out her skirt. She reminded herself again that she hated skirts, or dresses, that they were entirely too easy. Any and all of them. Hooker short, fashionably sexy, or long and elegant, she detested everything about them. Jeans, or loose-fitting sweats, were her comfort clothes. And of course, her puffy socks with her legs curled beneath her with her laptop perched on her legs and her fingers flying over the keys to spill out the stories clawing through her mind daily. She adored her seclusion and the multiple lives she got to live through every single character. And right now, she was in love with this skirt. It was going to look pretty draped over Vic's head.

When the waitress walked away, Ashley sipped the delicious wine and eyed her over the rim. Would they be fucking before the stroke of midnight? Would it be sinful to cast a desperate prayer for that very thing?

Sinful or not, she wanted Vic. Wanted her sprawled between her thighs, finger fucking while lapping her clit, drawing out mewls and pants of pleasure. Her nipples pebbled and her pussy throbbed with the thought.

Vic pulled her chair closer and leaned toward Ashley. "Did I tell you how much I enjoyed your reading? Humor and sex all rolled into one." She leaned closer and lowered her voice into a husky whisper. "Especially the sex."

Ashley swallowed and tightened her grip around the glass. Did she just moan out loud? Was she breathing? "Of course. Just."

Nobody had ever spoken about her work in those terms before. Hell, she'd never actually discussed her work with anybody face-to-face besides her best friend, Caprice, who herself was a best-selling erotic vampire author. In fact, other than a few short businesslike e-mails from the editor of the anthology no one had probably even known she existed until today's reading. And to think she'd almost begged off at the last minute terrified at the prospect of having to speak those sexy words in front of an audience.

Vic's mouth curled into that bewitching smile and Ashley was positive her body temperature spiked. "I have to admit, my favorite line was about the blond bombshell's IQ being the size of a slug. I think I dated her."

Ashley coughed and somehow kept her wine from spewing into Vic's face. "Then we have something in common already. Seems we have the same ex. She inspired that very line."

Vic chuckled and cupped her glass in one strong hand for a long, drawling sip. "Are you a full-time writer?"

Ashley wished beyond wishes she could nod. Fact was, her full-time job wasn't anything as glamorous as being a full-time writer, or traveling across the map for book signings. "I write in my spare time. I'm actually a financial planner for Strobe Brothers and work mostly from home."

"Nice. Not too shabby at all. However, the world would be much better off with more of your imagination on the market." Vic caressed the stem of her glass.

Ashley watched the motion and then felt the motion deep in her core. She reminded herself she was in public and took another sip. "Thank you. Too bad for the world that New York doesn't agree. They're tough as nails. Makes my tightwad bosses look like a couple of gay guys engaged in a handbag fight."

Vic threw her head back and laughed and Ashley found her gaze tagged on her throat. She envisioned her tongue traveling along every corded muscle, nipping none too gently as she pumped her fingers deep inside Vic.

Vic tapped her finger on the table. "Hey, that could be deadly. Try getting between a cross-dresser and a Gucci sale. It's not pretty." That fucking smile stretched Vic's lips once again.

Ashley crossed her legs and willed her self-control back in check. This was getting ridiculous, and she could barely cope with all this lust, or all that damn heat spiking across her pussy. "Well there's a thought. I could bus the cross-dressers to New York's doorstep and announce that the first one to snag me a contract wins a Gucci handbag and matching Mary Janes."

Vic laughed so hard heads turned their way. Ashley couldn't help but delve in the moment with a few giggles. "Oh, you're asking for a bloodbath, for sure. But with spunk like that, I don't see you giving up anytime soon. I look forward to reading your first novel."

Ashley rolled her eyes playfully. "Yeah, hold your breath for that one. I can draw a map of the USA, Canada, and Mexico in the inches of dust my manuscripts are collecting. All one of them." She didn't dare admit she had twenty more that she couldn't end because parting with her characters was like death. They seemed damned determined to hang on tight and never let go, or Ashley to them. She wasn't really sure anymore. Soon. Soon, she'd give them all the perfect ending then shoot them out into cyberspace with a few words of prayer.

Vic scooted closer. "Give them time. It'll happen. I feel it."

I've got something you can feel, and touch, and smell, and please, God, taste. "Glad someone feels it."

Vic thumbed the back of her hand on the table and Ashley practically jerked out of her chair. Her heart skimmed against her rib cage.

"So, Vic, what pays your bills?"

"I'm a chef."

"Wow. She's sexy *and* quenches appetites. In more ways than one, I'm sure." *Kill me. Just kill me now. Please tell me I didn't just say that out loud.*

Amusement flashed in Vic's mousse-colored eyes. "Hmm, more ways than one? I see the author has quite the imagination."

Embarrassed by her faux pas, Ashley dropped her gaze. But not enough imagination to solve yet another enigma. An ordinary chef wasn't likely to frequent a place like this, somewhere reserved for the rich and famous—unless she was a celebrity chef, and Ashley thought she knew all those from her research. And from what she'd read in the newspapers, a Victor Hadley was the chef and owner of this particular restaurant, so it was out of the question that she'd be a chef here. Regardless, celebrity or not, Vic certainly knew how to charm the birds from the trees and have them eating out of her hand in no time.

Thankfully, the waitress arrived with a large tray. She opened a tray holder and began filling their bowls with tossed salad.

Ashley practically spilled her silverware all over the table in an attempt to remove it from the linen napkin, anything not to look at Vic. She'd see the want, the thriving need, written all over her face and be forced to drop to her knees beneath this table like a hooker in a truck stop.

Fuck, she was acting desperate, like a sex-starved nymphomaniac. Hell, come to think of it, wasn't she? Weren't the characters in her stories the only people banging the headboards in her life?

When the waitress walked away, Vic scooted yet closer and their thighs touched. Ashley shoved a forkful of lettuce into her mouth, sparks of warmth thrashing across her crotch.

Vic rubbed a burning path up her thigh with her finger. Ashley moaned, unable to trap the sound. When she looked up, Vic was staring at her, something sinful dancing in her eyes. Ashley waved her fork around the edge of her bowl and mumbled around her food. "Sorry, couldn't help it. This is incredibly delicious. Absolutely mouthwatering."

Vic's brow rose. "Don't think I've ever heard anyone moan that loud over a salad. I'll have to give my compliments to the chef before we leave."

Ashley nodded, chewing wildly, her insides cramping tight. "Yes, please, this is to die for." *Jesus, this was so not the mark I wanted to leave. I'm weak, and easy.*

A few more inches with that damn finger and she wasn't going to allow Vic to reverse the path. A few more inches and the fact they were in a public place wouldn't matter, she'd be begging Vic to finger fuck her beneath this table, whether she liked it or not.

Vic pulled her hand away as if she'd read Ashley's mind, that anything further was dangerous territory. Ashley breathed a sigh.

By the time the main course arrived, the first bottle of wine was finished and a second stood open and ready. Vic refilled her glass and Ashley practically sucked it down like a wino on a drinking binge. Fuck, this was not the way grown adults were supposed to act. Okay, fine, so she was the only one acting like this, but she had a shrewd feeling that Vic knew she was causing a heated frenzy in Ashley right now. Those delicate caresses on her hand, arm, thighs… oh yeah, she knew what she was doing and she was enjoying every second of the tension she was generating.

Ashley willed her nerves back into some kind of normal function and focused on the delicious meal. Thick prime rib patted with horseradish, asparagus spears mixed with wild mushrooms dabbled with a butter garlic sauce, and a broiled tomato, cut water lily style, lay like a masterpiece upon the square white plate—the perfect natural aphrodisiac.

She wasn't sure where to start first. Everything looked too damn pretty to devour, and her stomach gave a silent growl in protest.

"Here, taste this." Vic held out a slice of pink beef, dark gravy dripping from the edge.

Ashley leaned forward, watching Vic under hooded lids, and took the morsel between her lips, every fiber in her body spiked with awareness of how intently Vic watched the movement. She closed her eyes and let the meat linger on her tongue for several seconds before it dissolved in her mouth.

Unable to stop herself, Ashley licked her lips and smiled. "Mmm, pink, tasty, and dripping with flavor, just the way I like it."

Vic raised a brow. "Pink always was my favorite color."

Ashley opened her mouth for the comeback then realized she only had one: *Please, fuck me now.* She couldn't dare let the plea slip past her lips.

Bite after delicious bite, they fed each other. Ashley doing more moaning and sighing than should be allowed in an elegant restaurant, or in public, and Vic entirely too close for her nerves to handle the closeness, seemingly unaware of the sounds.

Ashley was positive she'd never wanted a woman as much as she wanted this one right now. Right here on the table, straddling her beneath the table, anywhere, she didn't care. The food, the stares, those inviting caresses, it was all too much and her body was on fire, her pussy clenching and unclenching like a clamshell.

"No more, please. I'm going to bust." Ashley wiped her mouth, gave a heavy sigh and looked up into those dark eyes.

And then Vic was leaning in, her eyes trained on Ashley's lips, something dominant and overpowering nestled in the depths of those eyes. From the strained expression, every sound had awakened something lethal in her.

Ashley strained toward Vic, wanting—yearning—for that kiss like she wanted nothing else in her life before. Without it, she was sure she'd explode and she didn't fucking care who the hell saw them.

Vic's lips touched hers. Ashley closed her eyes. The incredible sensation had her floating on air, too dreamy to think. Soft. Dear God, her lips were so soft, like silk, and she could smell the wine against her breath as Vic pressed harder. She teased Ashley for several agonizing seconds, rubbing her mouth back and forth, her wine-scented breaths nothing more than puffs of hot air against her cheek and mouth. Just when Ashley was positive she was going to grab a handful of hair and demand that kiss, Vic sealed their lips together and slicked her tongue inside.

Ashley almost reeled back from the emotion. Her gut cramped and her pussy was so tight it physically hurt. Desperation pricked along her skin as Vic wove her fingers around the nape of her neck to pull her closer.

Fuck almighty, she was an author, and for the first time in her life, she couldn't describe how her body suddenly enflamed with life. Her mind was completely void of anything coherent, yet her body was alive.

Heaven help her, her body was so fucking alive.

CHAPTER FOUR

Vic was out of control, yet completely in control. Ashley's mouth was so sweet, so enticing. Her tongue probed deeper, searching for that special contact that made her shiver with desire. She'd never felt anything so powerful and conflicting in her entire life. She struggled not to drag Ashley out of the chair onto the floor to fuck her. She owned this place, for crying out loud. What would her customers think of her? Her staff? Hell, what did they think already? There's no telling what Elena had to finagle to free up the corner table on such short notice. Vic made a silent vow to make her Christmas bonus extra fat this year.

And poor Beth. Vic had barely been able to keep a straight face when she came to take their order, shocked to see her boss in the company of a woman. Her employees rarely saw her dating, let alone on a date in her very own restaurant. Actually, it'd never happened before. Sure, they knew she was gay, even teased her about setting her up with one friend or another, but never once had she dined a female in her place of employment—no matter if she owned the joint.

Maybe it was smug and egotistical of her to bring Ashley here, but she couldn't help herself. She wanted Ashley on her own terms, on her own terrain. She wanted to woo her with the glitz and glamour her sweat and blood had earned her. But why she needed Ashley to be the first, she didn't know. Why did she need to dazzle her?

Ashley gave a soft whimper when Vic deepened the kiss and

she practically unraveled. What was Ashley doing to her? Whatever it was, it'd begun from the second she stood tall, all five feet maybe five inches of her, in front of that wobbly card table back at the small downtown bookstore and spoken the first erotic word.

It hadn't stopped since.

And right now, Vic was beside herself with an insatiable need. It was curling through her body like ribbons of heat, twisting her gut into tight knots, and damn if she wasn't moaning as well.

She pulled away, too afraid of what she might do if things didn't slow down, yet also of what she might not do before her time ended with this beauty. The thought of missing anything, like not exploring every single inch of Ashley's delectable body or drawing a quiver or scream of pleasure from her lips, nearly destroyed her sanity.

She wanted her fingers, hands, mouth, body, all wedged between Ashley's thighs at the same time. Wanted her bellowing her name as she came so fucking hard.

Sweat. She wanted to feel her sweat and pump. And go on pumping until they were both drained.

Damn, where could they go?

Office? No. It was too far away and the route too public. Besides, it was too close to the kitchen. That's all she needed was her employees witnessing her locking the door behind a gorgeous female.

She couldn't do what she wanted on the damn table, though the scene had crossed her mind a few dozen times while feeding Ashley all those succulent tidbits. At this point, she was almost willing to take her chances on her own staff calling the cops on her for indecent exposure. A conviction of lewd acts in public would definitely shoot her business into the ground, but it might be worth it just to hear Ashley Vaughn cry her name.

God! She screwed her eyes shut. What was she doing even thinking the unthinkable? She hadn't known Ashley more than a few hours and yet here she was giving in to uncontrollable, obsessive lust and allowing it to rule her thoughts and drive her insane.

The bubbling hot need was too much to bear. She was

coming apart at the seams, her whole body in thrall of Ashley. Her predicament worsened when she finally dragged her lids open and saw her own want mirrored in Ashley's eyes. There was no further thought.

Bathroom! Now!

As gently as she could, she grabbed Ashley's hand and lured her from the chair, down the darkened hall, and into the bathroom. Vic thanked her guardian angel that the room was unoccupied.

Past the long wall of sinks with sparkly clean mirrors and marble floors, she wrenched Ashley into the farthest stall and slammed the door shut behind her.

Ashley's fingers fisted into her hair before she could wedge her against the tiled stall wall. She pulled Vic's head back and licked her throat, her tongue sweeping seductively across the skin as if it were a hot fudge temptation and she'd thought of nothing else all night.

Vic growled and grappled with her skirt while Ashley's fingers tugged at her shirt, her panting deep and throaty.

She hiked the hem up around Ashley's waist, then palmed her hand against her crotch.

Ashley whipped her head against the wall and let loose a sharp cry. The sound echoed around the empty bathroom and penetrated Vic's ears like a tribal drum beat.

She released an animalistic sob to feel how hot and wet Ashley was.

"Damn, you're wet and so ready." Vic wove her fingers around the string of her thong and slicked a single digit along her slit, dragging it forward until she tagged her pebbled clit. "Oh, God, you're so ready."

Ashley ground her lean hips against Vic, her fingers tightened in the strands of her hair. "Oh…fuck, yeah."

Vic tried to slow things down, but her need was too strong. She braced herself then drove two fingers inside Ashley. Her insides gripped the digits and Vic's pussy spasmed.

Godammit, she'd never felt anything so intense in her fucking life. She'd never wanted to fuck someone so bad, or needed to fuck them so hard. The reading had woken her animal lust. That was it.

It had to be the reading, the characters clinging to one another, with Vic placing herself and Ashley in the slots.

Ashley's arms tightened around her shoulders and her nails dug into her spine. Vic hissed and welcomed the sweet pain, then pumped into her, lifting Ashley clear off the floor with every harsh thrust.

She fucked her, driving up and into her, reaching the very depths of her core. Ashley's slick walls grabbed at her, tightening around her, sucking her in deeper.

"Vic, I'm gonna…" Ashley whimpered.

Vic withdrew from her. "Oh no, you don't, Speedy Gonzales. It's not time."

The disconnection snapped Ashley from her trance. She blinked then scrambled at Vic's belt before unsnapping her slacks. She tugged like a wild woman on a mission. When Vic's pants fell around her ankles, Ashley clawed at her briefs and pulled them down her legs, slowly kneeling with every inch they lowered.

Christ, those eyes watching her with her descent, so fucking gorgeous.

It was all Vic could do not to pull her back to her feet, drape her over the stainless steel toilet, and fuck her relentlessly.

Instead, she braced herself against the back wall while Ashley thumbed her lips apart and slicked her tongue against her beaded clit.

She dug her head against the wall while Ashley lapped at her, dragging her tongue in slow, easy glides along her most sensitive spot.

Her hips instinctively jerked and she dug her hands in Ashley's hair.

"You taste good." Ashley tongued her slit, those eyes daring Vic to come.

Vic could stand no more. She jerked Ashley to her feet, roughly spun her around, and pressed her cheek against the cold steel.

She pumped against her ass, kissing her cheek and neck, then drew back to watch Ashley's lips part, all while wondering why Ashley hadn't described this gnawing need in her reading. The uncontrollable yearning, the drenching want, those were the things that should have been featured inside those pages. Not that Vic could describe the emotions choking her right now, but she wasn't an author who could paint the perfect picture with a keyboard.

Oh, but Ashley could. Yet, she hadn't.

Maybe she hadn't experienced this kind of blinding desperation before. Highly unlikely, but possible.

When Ashley reached back and probed between her legs, Vic widened her stance. She shoved the hem of Ashley's skirt up around her heart-shaped ass then tore the thong down her legs.

"I'm going to fuck you, Ms. Ashley Vaughn."

Ashley whimpered, her eyes screwed tight. "Please, I beg you. I've thought of nothing else all night."

Vic pulled her hair away from her neck and worked her throat like a vampire, sucking, kissing, and nibbling her way down across a slender shoulder. She wedged her fingers between Ashley's parted thighs until she found her creamy opening, then drove inside her.

Ashley cried out and pushed backward against her, her fingers working into the vee of Vic's crotch, farther still until she parted through her slick lips. Vic wanted to mount her, wanted to drive her over the brink until she floated back down, then start again. Fuck, she was so twisted it was whiplashing.

They fingered and fucked each other, breathless, wild with need, and out of their minds with their oncoming orgasms.

Ashley bucked backward while Vic thrust forward, both in perfect unison until Vic felt the biting sting of her orgasm.

The bathroom door creaked open and women's chatter filled the room.

Ashley stopped, but Vic couldn't dream of halting her steady penetration. She was too far gone, too out of control to need anything other than Ashley pumping around her fingers. Two stalls toward the front opened and closed while Vic thrust inside her.

When Ashley attempted to turn around, Vic pinned her harder against the wall. She pressed her lips against Ashley's ear and whispered. "I can't fucking stop, Ashley. Give me your lips so I can taste the sound of you coming."

Ashley froze and then her insides convulsed. Vic closed her mouth around her lips, taking in every moan, every whimper, and every sound. Ashley bucked backward, fucking herself over Vic's fingers, her orgasm squeezing with robust contractions.

Vic had never experienced anything so erotic, so overwhelming, or so fucking hot. She held on tight while a toilet flushed, and then another. She lightly flicked Ashley's clit until she went limp and sagged in her arms. Vic tightened her grip and held her firmly against the wall to keep her from spilling to the floor.

Neither spoke while the women's chatter faded, Ashley's breathing subsiding into dull inhales.

Vic closed her eyes and nestled her face into the crook of her neck. She smelled like sex, and wildflowers. She smelled content.

"That was...wow, well, yeah, that was something." Ashley chuckled and began a lazy circle motion against Vic's clit, her body still lightly trembling.

Vic jerked, her clit was a ball of flames, giving new meaning to the phrase "blue balls," definitely provoked by Ashley's shattering orgasm and the intensity of the moment.

Just when Vic thought she could handle no more of the painful flicks, Ashley looked over her shoulder. "It's your turn. Come for me, Vic." Ashley pinched her clit and Vic shattered. Her orgasm washed over her in reckless waves of wet heat.

Ashley wedged her fingers farther until she found Vic's soaked opening, then drove inside.

Vic clutched at her, her insides pumping so hard she feared she'd burst vital organs. She could feel Ashley's body grinding against her, those fingers arching backward, thrusting inside her, the palm of her hand massaging her clit, keeping her riding the waves of pleasure.

"Harder, Vic. Faster, please." Ashley thrust backward and it was then Vic realized her fingers were still buried inside her, keeping perfect rhythm with Ashley's thrust.

While her body quivered, she lowered her other hand to Ashley's crotch and flicked her clit.

"I'm coming, Vic. Fuck, I'm coming!" Ashley drove her head

against Vic's shoulder and then her body shook like the fronds of a palm tree in a fierce storm.

Vic was vaguely aware of Ashley begging for God, and panting Vic's name, her whole body tense and vibrating.

Vic held tight to her as she thrashed about, pumping her fingers deep, her own orgasm still throbbing, and finally, they both slumped against the wall.

She wanted to move, yet never wanted to move again. She had Ashley pressed against a bathroom wall, her fingers still buried deep inside her wetness, with her pussy still clenching in tight spasms.

Ashley had just come around her fingers twice, she had just made Vic come, and she felt so fucking good, Vic never wanted to leave this bathroom.

The bathroom.

Christ, she couldn't have chosen a more disgusting place to make love to someone as fine as Ashley?

She suddenly felt cheap, or rather, that she'd treated Ashley so cheaply. The price of the meal, or even the two bottles of wine, couldn't justify dragging Ashley to a fucking bathroom, of all places.

And worse, if she never saw her again, the memory would forever torment her.

Every time she came here, every single day from now on, she'd see this place and remember.

CHAPTER FIVE

Ashley floated down slowly from her rushed high, unbelievably unsatisfied. She wanted and needed more. So much more.

Her insides ached pleasantly. She should be satisfied from the powerful orgasms, and yet her body still craved more.

The weight of Vic's body felt so good against her back. Incredible. All of it. The wildness, the overbearing need—she'd never encountered anything like it.

When Vic eased away from her, Ashley felt the loss. She turned around, her legs weak as water, and leaned against the cold tile for support.

Before she could say something, anything, Vic closed the gap and gently pressed their lips together. Her tongue slid along her bottom lip before slipping into her mouth.

Ashley tried to trap the moan but the damn thing rushed into Vic's mouth before she could silence it. Vic matched the sound and deepened the kiss, not nearly as wild as before. This time caressing, sweet, and oh so fucking gentle.

"Come home with me, Ashley," Vic whispered and rested her forehead against Ashley's, her eyes pleading. "This wasn't enough."

No longer tipsy from the wine, and past the adrenaline rush, Ashley nodded. She wanted nothing more than to spend the night in Vic's arms, in her bed, to come once, twice, or many times again by her hands.

Vic smiled like the cat that got the saucer of cream all to herself. She took Ashley's hand and led her out of the confined stall, out of the bathroom, past the table where they'd shared their first kiss, and out into the night. Ashley wasn't surprised to find the sidewalk still crowded with anxious people, most decked to the nines, their chatter non-important as Vic whisked her past them to the curb.

It suddenly occurred to her that Vic hadn't picked up the check. She tugged her hand until Vic stopped and turned around. "You aren't stiffing the restaurant, are you?"

Vic grinned and shook her head. "Of course not. It's taken care of."

Ashley didn't believe her. Good fuck or not, she didn't want to be banned from a restaurant she'd probably never step foot back inside. Or be hunted down like a criminal because her date was too damn cheap to pay. "Bullshit."

Vic stepped closer and took her other hand, staring down over her with those brilliant eyes. "I promise. I didn't stiff anyone."

"Then how do you explain leaving without paying?"

"Let's just say I have a tab here."

"Like hell you do." She crossed her arms and glared. "Either you go back in there and pay the bill or I will."

Vic trailed a single finger down her arm. "Trust me. It's been taken care of."

Ashley raised her chin defiantly, seriously considering going back inside. Something in Vic's calm stare kept her from doing so. "Why should I? I barely know you."

An incredulous smile crept across those lips. "You know what I sound like coming. Isn't that enough?"

Fuck. There comes the heat again. Ashley looked away, pissed that Vic could make her blush like a virgin bride not once, but more times than she could count anymore.

"That has nothing to do with the subject at hand, now does it?"

"Depends on which hand we're using."

Ashley playfully pushed her hand away, too conflicted to know what to do. Her mind told her to go back inside and do the right thing. But her gut told her Vic wasn't lying.

"I own Ellirondos."

Ashley widened her eyes and took a step back, sure now Vic was lying. What kind of sick freak acted like this, took women on dinner dates, and then raced them away before the check arrived? Was she a homeless bum? Damn fine as hell, either way, but still, she couldn't stand the thought of being a fugitive over a pricey dinner... and a good fuck. Ashley suddenly felt cheap, and her heart drooped a little. Up to this point, her date with this gorgeous woman had been immaculate, a night she wouldn't forget for many years to come. It was obvious she was going to be footing the bill for her dining pleasures, and an excellent fuck.

"Yeah, right, and I'm Angela Knight."

A quizzical stare crossed Vic's face. "Who's Angela Knight?"

Ashley rolled her eyes. "Only the hottest erotic vampire writer ever known to mankind, that's who. Well, besides my best friend, that is."

"I don't read vampire books. Hell, I barely read at all."

Ashley shifted to her other foot. "Oh really? Then why were you in the bookstore today?"

"To meet you."

A band of heat ran the length of Ashley's body. She lowered her gaze to the cobblestone sidewalk, gathered her wits, and then looked back into Vic's face. "That's sweet, and a crock of shit. Now, are you going to take your ass back inside to pay the bill or do I have to?"

A grin broke out along Vic's lips then she turned toward the valet standing on the curb. "Phillip, could you tell the lady my name, please?"

The young boy turned around, his sea green eyes staring between Vic and Ashley. "Ma'am?"

Ashley chuckled, but anger bubbled. *How dare the bitch do this.* Ashley couldn't wait to get home to a hot shower where she could scrub her skin into red welts.

"My name, Phillip. Tell her."

"Victoria. Victoria Hadley."

Ashley jolted with the name and whipped her head up to look at him, then turned to Vic who wore an appeased smile.

"Thank you," Vic said then looked down at Ashley. "There. Are you satisfied?"

"Victor Hadley…that's the chef here, right?"

"Nope. Gotta love the reporters and their typos. I am Victoria Hadley and indeed the occasional chéf, and the owner. I promise, the staff was well tipped for their prompt actions to secure us that table." She lowered her voice into a husky whisper and pressed closer to Ashley's ear. "Well worth it, I might add."

Ashley felt the heat dominating her neck once again and was terribly thankful their night wouldn't come to a screeching halt after all. She desperately needed more time with her sexy date.

With her unsettled wits back in check, they waited for her car. Vic stood tall beside her, her hand resting reassuringly against the curve of Ashley's back. She was so sexy, and Ashley felt a gripping bite of anxiety. This wasn't in her character to be going home with a stranger, even one as sexy as Vic. Or one as obviously important. A five-star restaurant. How freaking cool was that? Better still, now she had an occupation to add to her character study sheet.

The valet slowed her car to a stop and Ashley jerked to attention, and then practically bolted off the curb in haste to get on with the rest of their evening. She needed Vic naked against her, their bodies entwined as one and grinding against one another, with Vic delving between her thighs, and making her sob from the intensity.

Tomorrow, she would paint the description onto the pages of her computer. This she was sure. Their night would be too incredible not to record. This might very well be her only chance to transcribe reality into the web of her mind and then into an incredible story for the world to see. Was it sick of her to want to let this evening breathe beyond this single night? And a single night it would be. She was sure Vic wasn't the type of woman who came back for seconds. Neither was Ashley. And her rush for success left no room to ponder such things as romance on a personal level. Actually, she never looked for love. It was a waste of time looking for something that didn't exist outside the pages of a novel or a movie script.

Vic escorted her to the car and opened the door. "My car's around the corner. Follow me?"

The look in her eyes was almost pleading. Ashley had no desire to do anything but follow Vic right now. Hell, with eyes making promises like that, she'd follow her to the end of a mineshaft with the detonator on the opposite end.

"Absolutely."

Vic smiled, closed the door behind her, and jogged down the sidewalk to disappear around the corner.

Ashley pulled away slowly, her body enflamed with need, her mind stroking back the details so far. Hell, based on one night alone, she could write a three-hundred-page novel, packed with intense sex, with a happily ever after to boot.

Of course, her time with Vic wouldn't end so happily. Love was an illusion. It was a myth created through the hands of authors, and tomorrow she was going to paint something just as spectacular. And this time, she wouldn't tuck the manuscript away, clinging to the characters like they were her own lovers. The manuscripts sucking up space on her hard drive wouldn't snag her a contract without an ending.

This time, she was positive she'd give her characters their deserved ending, and then, with her head held high, she was going to send them into cyberspace and beg for patience. And pray for a contract.

Ashley rounded the corner to find Vic ducking into a Spider Eclipse. The sporty little car seemed to fit her—sleek and sexy, yet fast and furious.

The ride to her house was anything but fast. She couldn't get there quick enough, nor was she shocked when Vic pulled into one of the new gated housing communities in Paradise Valley.

Not soon enough, she swung into the driveway of a two-story mocha-colored stucco house, the norm for Arizona, another reason Ashley vowed to move far, far away. She wanted green grass and tall trees that waved in the gentle breeze instead of cactus and birds to wake her with the morning light. She was tired of the heat and dust, the barren desert with most houses matching its dullness, and rocks. Sheesh, there were only so many boulders a girl could take.

She parked beside Vic's expensive ride and climbed from the car, scanning the front of the house, already impressed to see Vic had deviated from the norm with the exterior by creating a series of ornamental archways, enclosing the area behind a glass screen to make a covered patio.

When Vic gave her that enchanting smile, she wanted to drag her inside, wanted to throw her on the floor and ride her. Ride her until they were both spent from multiple orgasms and energy.

Fuck! She'd never been so horny in her life, even after the fierce orgasms ripped from her less than an hour ago.

"It's not much, but I call it home," Vic announced as Ashley beeped her doors locked and followed her onto the covered patio.

Ashley hid her eye roll at the comment. Leave it to someone with a fat bank account and a two-story mini-mansion to call it "not much."

Vic unlocked the front door while Ashley composed herself. Beyond those doors was an entire house of privacy, perfect for all the moans and sharp cries she needed Vic to pluck from her body.

Ashley barely had enough time to take in the large open living area with a two-story cathedral ceiling while Vic closed and locked the door. With the lock engaged, Ashley turned and latched on to her, trapping her against the oak, her mouth sealing, and her tongue searching.

Vic released an animalistic growl then palmed Ashley's ass, drawing her legs up around her waist.

She walked several paces into the room then started up the wide staircase that led to a circular gallery that overlooked the great room. Halfway up, Vic eased her down onto one of the treads, her body wedging between Ashley's parted thighs. Ashley moaned when she hiked her skirt up around her stomach, and her pussy drenched, weeping with need.

Fuck, what was it about Vic? There was something, that was for sure, but damned if Ashley could put her finger on it. She desperately wanted that piece of information. She knew whatever it was, it was critical.

Vic draped Ashley's leg over her shoulder and slid down a step until she was facing her crotch. "You ready to be fucked, Ashley Vaughn?" She licked the seam of her thong wedged against her pussy and Ashley flew apart.

She sucked in a breath, fisted one hand in Vic's hair, the other searching for refuge on a spindle for support.

"Such dainty little panties you have here. And they're in my fucking way."

Ashley whimpered and thrust her hips forward, her pussy on fire. "Hell! I don't care how, just get rid of them."

Vic smiled, winked, wrapped her fingers around the string and ripped them off Ashley's body, then dove in, her mouth working Ashley's clit as if it were an Olympic sport.

Ashley pumped her hips, wildly driving her pussy against Vic's mouth.

When Vic withdrew, Ashley groaned, opened her eyes, and met Vic's heated expression. "Take off your clothes. I want you naked."

Ashley's nipples pebbled against her push-up bra. Her hands shook as she slowly worked the skirt and blouse up her back and over her head. Vic's intense gaze watching her every move set hot talons clawing at her core.

When the clothes hit the stair above her head, Vic swept that sexy tongue along her slit as a reward. Ashley gasped, her pussy pulsing against Vic's mouth. Vic nodded for the bra then drew on her clit for reassurance.

Ashley obeyed, unsure how much more she could take before she combusted. Every fiber in her body already fluttered with life.

With slow, yet nervous fingers, Ashley slid the straps down her arms, flipped the catch, and let the bra fall on the stairs beside her.

While those rich, dark eyes watched her, Ashley did something she'd never done or even dreamt of doing before. She cupped each breast, squeezing and molding them. She knew she should feel like a wanton hussy, but for some reason, she didn't. This night was like no other. Tonight, Vic's influence had given her freedom to please herself and damn the consequences. Besides, the way Vic was eating her alive in that carnal stare, who would want, or have the strength, to pass up such a moment?

When Vic drew her clit between her lips, Ashley threw her head back and bucked toward that pleasing mouth. Her nipples ached for attention—for Vic's attention.

Vic's breaths quickened against her skin, hot and ragged. Ashley pinched her nipples and something electrifying shot down her spine.

As if Vic knew it was too much, that Ashley was so close it was painful, she draped Ashley's other leg over her shoulder then shoved both legs toward Ashley's chest.

Ashley cried out. As her body opened up fully and her wall of reserve shattered, she pumped and twisted, her mind too full, her pussy too hot. And then her orgasm jerked her body into spasms, wave after wave of liquid fire consuming her.

And then Vic was there, hovering over her like a fucking barbarian goddess, her fingers buried deep, thrusting, pumping, and reaching the very depth of Ashley's soul.

It was all too overwhelming and too intense. Her body ached and pulsed with the most excruciating pleasure she'd ever experienced.

She was vaguely aware of digging her nails into the wood, crying Vic's name, of hot tears stinging her lids, pumping so damn hard around those fingers.

Vic hissed and arched backward as Ashley dragged her nails down her back in search of something solid to clamp onto, finally palming her ass, pulling her closer, and deeper.

The spasms finally subsided when Vic withdrew her fingers. Ashley fell back, drained, boneless, and sucking in shallow breaths.

Vic removed Ashley's death grip on the stair tread and draped her arms around her own neck. "Hold on, baby."

She wrapped her arms around Ashley's body and lifted her from the floor.

Ashley clung to her like a limpet to a rock until Vic placed her on a soft surface, unwound her arms from her neck, and withdrew. Feeling deserted, Ashley's eyes flicked open, searching to locate Vic, and she found herself in the center of a wide bed, a bed fit for a king. A high, pale wood headboard stocked with books, mainly cookbooks plus a few select romance novels from what she could see, rested against a creamy, moss green wall. She fingered a matching leaf pattern on the thick cream comforter beneath her and quickly wondered how many other woman had lain in this exact spot, or how many other women had just come screaming on that staircase.

Before she had time to develop that thought, Vic prowled across the mattress and eased between Ashley's thighs. "Do you know how breathtaking you look against this bed with your dark hair fanned out around you?" She licked Ashley's bottom lip then ducked to the hollow of her throat. "Good enough to eat, Ms. Vaughn. Again."

Ashley squirmed, her body responding eagerly to Vic's touch. It was amazing, really, how every nerve in her body was alive with sensitivity. She pondered the reason why. It wasn't like she'd never had a one-night stand before, or one who hadn't fucked her mercilessly, but this one, oh man, this was giving new meaning to cataclysmic sex.

Before Vic could entrance her again, Ashley shoved at her chest until she fell over on her back. Instead of climbing over to straddle her, she tugged her belt loose and dragged the slacks down those delectable legs. Encased in tighty whites, Vic looked more enticing than any Ralph Lauren model.

Ashley licked a path up the inside of her leg, nipped the edge of her briefs, and then tugged them with her teeth. "These are in my way."

Vic grinned, that damn dimple indenting on her left cheek. "Can't have that, now can we?" She lifted her hips while Ashley dragged the briefs down and tossed them on the floor.

She climbed farther until she straddled Vic then pulled at the seam of her shirt. "This, off, now!"

Vic slowly rose, tugging the shirt down her arms. Just when Ashley thought she was going to shed the material, Vic grabbed her waist and rolled her onto her back.

"Dammit!" Ashley tried to pretend defeat. Fact was, she really liked rocking beneath Vic's weight. "If I didn't know any better, I'd swear you were playing hard to get." She ran her finger down a knotted muscle on Vic's arm. "By the way, you now have my autograph."

"Oh really? How so?"

"My claw marks stamped down that sexy back of yours." Ashley winked and pulled Vic down.

Vic sucked at her neck. "It was the sweetest pain I've ever felt. And in response to your other statement, I *am* hard to get. Just easy for *you* to catch."

Ashley didn't know what to say, wasn't sure Vic had meant the statement quite as sweetly as it'd come out.

Vic moved to the side as she shucked out of her shirt and sports bra, one leg cocked over Ashley's. Ashley circled her breasts then lightly pinched her nipples. Vic was incredible in every sense of the word: perfect handfuls of breasts, dark nipples crying to be sucked, and her body athletic and tight. It was enough to make a grown woman cry.

She grabbed Ashley's hand and wedged it between their bodies, down between her legs. "Catch me, Ashley."

Ashley licked her lips as words from her short story came to mind. "I thought you'd never ask."

Chapter Six

Ashley stared beyond the silken strands of Vic's hair to the large dark window, her mind numb and her body weak from so much sex, from so many orgasms. Vic's arm lay across her stomach, pinning her to the bed, and her body was like a soft cloak against her side. Her breathing had settled into a steady balance, no more than a warm zephyr brushing against Ashley's neck.

The low-watt bedside lamp cast soft shadows across the bed. Ashley turned to face Vic. She watched her eyes dance behind her closed lids. What a great lover she'd been. She couldn't believe how many times Vic's name had left her lips—torn out of her soul in an orgasmic scream or in soft gasps of indescribable pleasure. She wanted to ponder if any other lover had ever done such acts but knew it was a waste of time.

As if Vic knew Ashley was watching her, she snuggled deeper into the crook of her arm and pulled Ashley tighter against her.

The gesture was sweet, really, and Ashley had a fleeting moment of contentment. If only love were real. It wasn't, of this she was sure. She'd searched for romance too many times throughout her life. And every time, just when she thought she could feel it in the palm of her hand, the wind carried it away, or rather, some fresher piece of ass lured it from her grasp.

She wasn't that bothered about her past relationships. Easy come, easy go. Though each and every one served as a reminder that lust was the real magic at work behind the burning desire that drove people into each other's arms and beds. Not love. Ashley could live with the facts. She liked living with cold, hard reality. Whims and fantasies were for the weak.

It suddenly occurred to her. Maybe that's why she held on to her characters with a death grip—because she couldn't square the happily ever after the world demanded, when in reality, there was no such thing. So why couldn't they have a happy for now ending? What was so wrong with that? Didn't it happen every day all around her?

She sighed and turned back to the window to focus on the night sky. That wouldn't work either. Women read her story because they wanted to experience the elusive cloak of happiness vicariously through the characters, to snag the impossible dream. They wanted to know the untamable had been caught and claimed.

Couldn't the readers see that sex was just that—sex? There didn't have to be doves and rose petals and happily ever after in the end. Just two women, completely satisfied, who could walk away in opposite directions when the lust had maxed itself out, with their heads held high, without bruised hearts or scorned feelings. Right?

Vic snuggled closer yet again, draping a leg across Ashley's like only intimate lovers should do. Fuck if it didn't feel good. And she smelled like sleep and sex. Nothing felt that good. Nothing.

She resisted stroking the hair back from Vic's face as she turned to find a sleepy smile playing against her lips. Fuck almighty if she wasn't sexy, and she fit the description of almost every butch in Ashley's novels. If she weren't a sane person, she could easily be fooled into thinking she'd found her soul mate, or something damn close. She was surely everything Ashley ever wanted in a woman: self-sufficient, hard working, independent, and fucking awesome between the sheets. If only she believed in such farcical fantasies. But she didn't. She was entirely too smart for that.

Vic tightened her grip around Ashley's stomach, curling those long fingers just beneath her breast. The weight across her rib cage suddenly felt too heavy, trapping her, and that fucking leg draped over hers was like a death trap. Her stomach knotted. Fuck, it was so heavy, like lead, pressing her against the soft mattress. Ashley drew in a breath, claustrophobia nipping at her mind. She tried to scoot out from under the pressure but Vic only clung tighter.

Fuck, fuck, fuck, she was going to suffocate right here in Vic's bed, with her body a mass of splendid soreness. She had to escape this weight or she'd go mad.

When Vic reached up to scratch her neck, Ashley seized her opportunity and rolled quickly to one side until she slipped off the edge of the bed, her knees making a dull thud as she landed on the carpeted floor. She held her breath as Vic moaned softly then shifted onto her back and crooked her arm around her head. Soon, her breathing returned to that of a sound sleeper.

Ashley rose slowly for fear of waking Vic, and stared down at her. She knew she wouldn't be able to say good-bye to her if she woke and tempted her with those eyes. She wouldn't be able to resist that dimpled smile or the lure of her arms and the promise of more incredible sex.

Her time with Vic was like no other. It was sex and wild lust. But like Cinderella, it was over. Within the hour, the sky would lighten with the dawn. The thought chilled her. She couldn't still be lying here in Vic's arms or standing beside her bed. She just couldn't.

Vic was gorgeous and perfect. Ashley allowed herself a few minutes to look over every uncovered naked inch of her from her face to her breasts, down over her flat stomach to her mound, and lower to the mahogany-colored sheets draped sensually around her legs. And for many glorious hours, Vic had been hers. But now it was over.

For a brief second, Ashley considered crawling back into the bed to curl beside her. She shook her head. It was just her mind overshadowing the sex, the awesome, knee-quivering, tear-jerking sex.

Without another thought, Ashley grabbed her discarded heels from beside the bed where Vic had eased them from her feet with careful kisses, and then she bolted for the staircase. Silently, she searched for her skirt, blouse, and bra then quickly shrugged into them. Her thong was history, destroyed by the impatient hands of a unique lover, and nowhere in sight.

She crept down to the first floor and scanned the wall beside the door for a security box. She found several blown-up pictures of Vic's restaurant in different stages of completion. Starting with the breaking of the ground, they lined back up the staircase. She couldn't make out all of them, nor was she about to climb those stairs again, so she turned back to her search and found the box. The icon glowed green. She heaved a sigh of relief. She wasn't sure what she'd have done had the alarm been set to trap her inside this house. Right now, she wanted out. She needed freedom from the walls that were closing in around her; she wanted to be beyond those doors where she could breathe fresh air without the reminding odor of their sex hovering around her.

With a final glance back up the staircase, she scrambled through the door, her heart thundering against her chest.

Barefoot, she raced to her car like the hounds from hell were after her, sucking in desperate gulps of air. Only when she was safely behind the wheel of her car, with the doors locked behind her, did she feel safe. She couldn't remember feeling so caged or so desperate for release in her entire life.

She cranked the car and immediately felt better, like she was back in control.

One last glance back at the house proved all was still dark. Not that she expected a woman like Vic to chase her. Of course, a woman like Vic wouldn't chase her. That was for teens and drama queens. Vic would move on to her next conquest before the sheets had time to cool.

She let the handbrake off then slowly backed out of Vic's driveway and headed toward the freeway, toward home. Toward freedom. Toward a new novel.

Chapter Seven

Ashley, where are you? Why won't you respond to my e-mails? Please tell me what I did that was so wrong. I'm going nuts here imagining all sorts of terrible things and I need you to put me out of my misery. I just want to know why you left the way you did. I know I sound like a stalker, but I promise, I'm not. Nor am I into U-Hauling. I just want answers, or another dinner. Or you in my bed one more time. I don't think that's too much to ask after what we shared. *wink*

Please write me back, if only to tell me to fuck off.
Vic

Vic read the e-mail over for the fifth time then took a deep breath, said a silent prayer, and hit send. She immediately regretted her action and wished there was some way to grab it back, like a handy un-send button, or at least a big red easy button.

"Idiot!" She shoved away from the computer desk and swiveled the chair around to face the floor-to-ceiling windows overlooking her back yard. "You sound fucking desperate and totally sick."

She knew it, had known it from the first, second, or even third e-mail she'd sent. But she couldn't help herself, and God help her, knowing how fucking pathetic she sounded never stopped her from sending another e-mail twenty-four hours after the previous one, despite Ashley's silence. Hell! The lack of response merely spurred her on, and made her plead all the harder for answers.

There was no logical reason for Ashley to bolt the way she had. She'd gone over and over that night, filtered every hour down to the minutes, then even down to the seconds, and still, nothing. Yet something had made Ashley run away, leaving Vic clinging to a pillow filled with her scent when she woke the next morning.

"What the fuck did I do so wrong?" She forked her fingers through her hair and slammed back in the chair.

She stared at the ceiling, images of their solitary night playing through her mind like a video clip set to permanent loop. For weeks now, Ashley had rendered her helpless. She'd give anything to swipe Ashley's image from her mind and move on. She'd tried. Fucking hell, how she'd tried. To no avail. Maybe if Ashley would answer a single e-mail, or even answer just one of her questions, she could find some kind of closure on the whole episode.

Who the hell was she kidding? Vic sighed; she knew that wouldn't be the case. One answer would lead her to want another, and then another, until finally she'd be back to sounding desperate. Just like she'd sounded in almost every e-mail she'd sent so far. Ashley must surely think she was psycho.

How could such an incredible night turn out to be so...so wasted?

Okay, so that was stretching things a bit. Regardless of the outcome, she wouldn't change a single minute with Ashley. Well, actually, yes, she would, starting with that stupid, selfish, driving force to the bathroom. How in the hell could she have done that? Ashley deserved something far more graceful than a fucking bathroom stall.

"Fuck!" Vic leaned forward on her elbows, staring down at her bare feet against the thick gray Berber carpet.

That was it. When Ashley finally had time to think, had time to realize she was worth more than the lousy bathroom stall Vic had given her, she'd hightailed it out of there without a single glance back. How could Vic blame her? Anyone else would have waltzed her off to a five-star high-rise hotel, wooed her, and pampered her, would have lavished her in wine while treating her to a hot tub overlooking the bright lights of downtown Phoenix. Or better, they would have flown her in a private jet to some Caribbean island to sip mai tais under a fanning frond.

Vic had blown her chances with Ashley from the second she wrenched her away from the table, from the very second she slung her against the tiled bathroom wall. She'd blown it. Simple. And now there was no way to fetch the minutes back, and she couldn't undo a single second of their time together.

It was over long before she had a chance to find out what it was about Ashley Vaughn that left her so dumbfounded and why she still wanted her so fucking badly despite her lack of returning e-mails. How in hell had she parked herself so firmly inside her mind?

With a low grumble, she spun back around to face the monitor. "Write me back, Ashley. Tell me something, anything. Please. My mind's a scrambled mess."

In the space of a few short hours, Ashley had taken over her consciousness, embracing it with ever tightening tentacles, controlling her thoughts like an insidious computer virus. The biggest question—why, or how, had Ashley gotten so deep, so fast?

❖

Ashley stared at Vic's latest e-mail. What was this one, fortysomething? She'd lost count at around thirty. If she hadn't looked into Vic's sane eyes, she would probably have feared for her privacy right now. But she had, and Vic was right, she wasn't a stalker, or crazy. Her e-mails weren't the ramblings of a psychopath. It was worse, much worse. She wanted answers.

If only she had the answers to give Vic. She'd searched in vain for the same from the second she'd broken every speed limit leaving Vic's gated community. Thank the Lord there hadn't been any cops around that night; they'd have locked her up for sure.

"What the hell do you want from me?" Ashley tapped her fingers on the edge of the laptop and reread the e-mail.

What, exactly, was Vic asking for besides another fuck? If only that were possible. It wasn't. She couldn't risk another night in Vic's bed. That wouldn't solve anything, and it would only lead to another, and surely into another, until she found herself consumed by fear and uncertainty. Always waiting for something or someone to force her palms open, to drop Vic into the hands of another. She was above lovers' games now. There were other more important things she needed to focus on. Things that didn't involve personal loss, hurt, and heartache.

Why couldn't Vic just let it go? Why couldn't she move on?

Her gut fluttered as she read the words once again. And what a sweet e-mail it was, like all the others. Sure, she wasn't very savvy with her words, but Ashley could read between the lines. Somewhere edged into the black and white were feelings. She could almost hear Vic's rich voice speaking them loud and clear, and heaven help her, it made her heart falter. Was she being a fool? Could their one-night stand develop into something more, something beautiful and permanent? No! She had to stop this, finish it finally before she got hurt. One carefully worded e-mail should do the trick and set her free.

Before she could change her mind, Ashley hit the respond button to compose a new e-mail.

Their night together had been amazing, tender then passionate, all starting with wild and uncontrollable. Passion had never been so strong. But it was just that—lust. Whatever Vic thought she felt, it wasn't real. It was her appetite for sex playing wicked jokes on her mind. Ashley wasn't going to play into its clutches. She couldn't take a chance on this being different from all the other times; the risk was just too great, and the outcome too scary.

Reality was sitting at the bottom of her screen—her newest novel. She was already several chapters deep into its plot. A plot that mirrored her single night with Vic.

Of course, against her better judgment, she was going to give those characters a happy ending, unlike the way she and Vic had parted ways. That's what the world wanted: girl getting girl, and girl keeping girl for eternity. It made her growl, but in order to snag a contract, she'd have to play by the editor's rules. Her role as an author was to satisfy the reader's desire for the elusive dream, the fantasy that sold millions of books every year. And she had to find a way to like it.

She focused on Vic's e-mail once again, the desperation woven into the words, and let her fingers fly across the keys.

> *Vic, sorry I haven't responded before now...been buried writing a new novel. I just wanted to say a belated thank you for a wonderful evening. All parts of it. *winks back**
>
> *I really had a great time. Wish I could take you up on your offer, but at this time, there's no room in my life for Friday night flings, or anything else. I'm sure you understand.*
>
> *If everything goes well, maybe one day I'll be back in the bookstore for another reading *crosses fingers**
> *Ashley*

Ashley fought back the urge to change the e-mail, or just downright delete it. Was it too formal? Was it to the point? Was the meaning clear? Would it be clear to Vic?

With her head held high, she closed her eyes on the film of tears, her finger hovering over the mouse. She took a deep breath and clicked it, winging Vic's answers into cyberspace.

Better to give Vic a portion of what she needed—the closure.

CHAPTER EIGHT

Vic strode into the bookstore and walked through several aisles, ignoring the prominently displayed bestsellers, until she reached her favorite place, the tiny lesbian section. She stood with her feet planted firmly, staring down at Ashley's first novel, *Vapor*. She couldn't count how many times she'd stood in this exact spot over the past few months, only to do this very thing: stare at the cover. She'd watched the copies dwindle down to nothing, get restocked, and then dwindle down again. Only two copies remained today. Ashley's book was obviously a hit. Scorn aside, she was proud for her, thrilled she'd reached a personal goal in life. She'd been there once, reaching for the rungs that seemed impossible to reach.

Bound in red with black lettering, *Vapor* screamed erotic. Reading Ashley's name was as far as she'd gotten. Vic didn't know why she couldn't bring herself to pick it up, or God forbid, read the back cover blurb, let alone the entire book.

She was being silly, she knew, but something told her being inside Ashley's mind might very well rip out what little sanity she had left. Not that she was very far from there now. Those heated scenes inside the cover were sure to spike her temperature and enflame her pussy. The fact that she'd been between Ashley Vaughn's thighs made matters even worse, made things lethal. She'd pulled erotic sounds from her lips, had her quivering, had her coming. It would be torture to have to, once again, place herself in the slot of the characters. She'd felt the reality pulsing against her mouth. Hell, it could easily send her back to those pathetic e-mails she was sure had made Ashley roll her eyes, or worse, laugh at her. She couldn't stand the thought of Ashley making fun of her genuinely desperate need for answers.

Two years had passed her by since Ashley's nice "fuck off" e-mail—the one that seemed too formal for Vic's liking, as if Vic were just short of some kind of Ashley Vaughn groupie, not someone who'd had her body arching and screaming long into the night. She still had that closure saved in her inbox, and still opened it way too often when Ashley appeared in her mind. It was the perfect way to keep her in check, to rein her back in when her body craved Ashley's touch.

She had to admit that the years had been difficult as she tried to convince herself that whatever could have been with Ashley had crashed and burned with the squealing of tires leaving Vic's house. Nothing more could ever become of it, though some nagging feeling kept her from knowing that to its full extent. She focused on work as much as possible and tried to enjoy the occasional fuck with Heather, her best friend with benefits. As hot as their sex was, nothing tilted her world the way her night with Ashley had. Nothing spun her fucking universe in the opposite direction the way the sound of Ashley coming had, and sometimes still did.

What terrified her more was not knowing if she'd find that gut-gnawing feeling again. Would she ever find that one person who changed her life, that one person who left her satiated, yet never satisfied? Ashley had been that special person even on such a short acquaintance. Vic was as sure as she could be on that point. Heaven help her, she didn't know why.

Vic shook her head. Fuck! She was thinking about her again. Why couldn't she stop? How did Ashley have the power to sneak inside her mind at any given time, even when she was making love to another woman? Hell, that was the worst time, yet that seemed to be her most favorite, like a constant reminder that she was wasting her time looking elsewhere, that sex couldn't, and wouldn't, ever be as satisfying with any other female. So far, she'd been proven correct.

Before she could change her mind yet again, Vic reached out and plucked Ashley's novel from the shelf. Hadn't she procrastinated long enough? She was proud of Ashley, dammit, no matter how scorned she was.

She hurried to the checkout and tossed the book on the counter.

The sales clerk gave her a smile, one far too bright to be just an ordinary greeting. The white tag on her ivory green smock said her name was Mandy. Her translucent blue eyes twinkled as she turned the book over and slid it under the scanner, pursing those strawberry-red lips into a thin line. "Great choice." She lowered her voice. "I've read this one. It's hot. According to her blog, another is coming out soon."

Vic returned the smile, unsure if the girl was femme, straight, bi, or just flirting with a woman who'd never pass for anything but butch. She resisted the urge to tell her that she'd fucked the icon, that she couldn't rip her out of her mind. Damn, what a fool she was. "Cool. I'll be on the lookout for it."

"You can fill out an e-mail alert so you'll get a notification when it arrives." The clerk batted sultry lashes and pointed to a leaflet on the counter, leaving no room for question as to what she was thinking, or wanting, or insinuating.

Vic ignored the unsubtle invitation from a woman who couldn't be a day over twenty-five and tossed the bills on the counter. "No, thank you. I'm a frequent shopper here." Vic didn't dare say she was an Ashley Vaughn addict, that she read her blog weekly just to stay close to her. From the recent "having a hard time writing today" or "work sucked this week—me and numbers aren't getting along" to questioning her bloggers about which sexual position was their favorite, every blog entry always had numerous pages of responses. And every entry kept Vic near her mind.

She swore she was going to stop reading them. One day she was positive Ashley's blog would delve deep into her personal life.

Tell how she and some new chick had breathless sex, or worse, how they might be planning a ceremony to unite them as one. The fear made her cringe every time she double-clicked Ashley's Web site, but never kept her from reading everything new on her pages.

She was pathetic and she knew it.

The sales clerk bagged the book and Vic walked as slowly as she could toward the exit, resisting the urge to look over her shoulder to find eyes locked on her. She could feel the woman penetrating her back with that sultry stare.

Several blocks away from the bookstore, Vic found a vacant bench and sat down. Anticipating food, pigeons fluttered to her seat from all around when she dropped the bag beside her. When none was offered, they quickly landed back on the sidewalk to continue their pecking and cooing, all the while keeping a hopeful eye on the bag.

She watched them for several minutes just to avoid holding Ashley's book in her hands, knowing the contact would be too electrifying.

When the pigeons finally decided nothing else was worth their attention, they scurried down the sidewalk toward a new arrival. Vic took the book out of the bag.

Vapor. She loved the title. It was sexy and eye-catching and had a mysterious feel to it.

She thumbed across Ashley's name and wondered how excited she'd been to get a contract. Vic wished she could have been there to help her celebrate, in more ways than one. Ashley had waited a long time for New York to finally open their doors to her awesome form of writing, to her descriptions carried over beyond the bedroom door.

Her heart quickened and her gut knotted. By now, Ashley was sure to have a steady girlfriend, someone else who was making her sweat with lust. So she hadn't bragged about it in her blog. That didn't mean one didn't exist.

The thought was too unbearable. Vic flipped the book over and scanned the back cover blurb.

Vapor wants it all: love, security, a family, her own restaurant, and she wants it with Keeley Nash, the very sexy and alluring lesbian erotic romance author.

Safely wrapped in a world of her own making, Keeley wants plotlines, seducing her victims into earth-shattering sex for life experiences to twist into her bestsellers.

Will Vapor be the wisp of an erotic lover in Keeley's book, or will Keeley discover a real life plotline far surpasses anything her imagination can dream up?

Vic shoved off the bench, her knuckles white with her grip around the book. "What the fuck!" Dumbfounded, she read the blurb again, her head suddenly thumping, and finally, she read it once again.

No fucking way!

She paced several steps in front of the bench. The pigeons hurried her way, hopeful she would drop them some morsels. They grouped around her feet in clusters, their cooing grating her nerves.

"Shoo!" She stomped her foot and they fluttered back to the next bench, a few lingering to watch her warily.

After several more paces, she dropped back down on the bench to stare at the back cover in shock.

There had to be a mistake, had to be some twisted explanation. But a gnawing feeling grabbed hold of her gut and was damned to let go. She knew. The truth was right there, plastered on the back cover for everyone in the whole goddamn world to see. It was her incredible night with Ashley, she was positive. Only God knew what she'd find inside the cover.

She tore open the book and leafed to the first page. Her stomach cramped as she read the first, second, and third pages. The setting began in a bookstore, just like the day she'd met Ashley for the first time.

Vic couldn't read any more. She slammed the book shut and took in several gulps of air.

How could anyone be so fucking cruel? Or heartless? Oh man,

no wonder Ashley hadn't responded to any of her e-mails. She was trying to find the words to ward Vic off before her true intentions were exposed. The bitch!

She suddenly felt cheap, and disgusted, and her skin itched like a layer of filth had been poured over her. After several sharp breaths, she reopened the book and flipped through to the second chapter, hating her action immediately. Things only got worse. Now she was staring into Ashley's description of her restaurant, of the restaurant this character dreamed would be hers one day. Seemed she was a wannabe chef in Ashley's make-believe, yet completely true, world.

"Jesus fucking Christ!" Vic growled and started pacing again. A few midday strollers gave her a questioning stare but she ignored them and kept moving steadily back and forth, sure she looked like a lunatic.

"That fucking bitch. How could she do this?" Vic jerked up the bag and stomped toward her car parked a few stores down against the curb.

As soon as she dropped into the driver's seat, waves of sick despair washed over her. Ashley had used her in the most despicable way possible. She hadn't run from anything. She'd gotten all she needed from their night. She'd needed visual images to paint the perfect color picture onto her computer screen—inspiration to fill the pages of her novel.

Humiliation ran through Vic's veins. All this time, wondering what she'd done wrong. All the mental head bashing she'd done, desperate to know why Ashley hadn't wanted her, had all been for nothing.

Ashley had gotten exactly what she wanted. Oh yeah, she'd fucking gotten it all right. She'd taken their night and used it to boost herself to the top of the rungs. What a fucking, cheating piece of scum she was.

With her heart drooping, and rage bubbling, Vic opened the book again, this time searching for the dedication. Maybe her answers would be there. Maybe Ashley would've written something, anything, to make this gut-gripping hurt go away.

She wasn't surprised to find a smug little comment in a single sentence across the top: *This is only the beginning.*

Vic could well imagine this book was truly only the beginning and felt a sickening sympathy for all the other poor schmucks out there who would fall prey to Ashley Vaughn's machinations.

All pleasure for Ashley's success vanished as Vic tossed the book into the backseat and revved the engine to life.

Ashley Vaughn was heartless, and cruel, and a fucking bitch.

She begged the heavens above that she'd never cross Ashley's path again. God help her if she did.

❖

Ashley darted inside the store alcove across the street from Ellirondos, her ponytail pulled tight through the loop of her baseball cap. Large sunglasses blocked the view of her eyes. A woman gave her a hard stare as she skirted past, tossing glances over her shoulder as she quickened her pace up the sidewalk.

"Sorry…so sorry." Ashley tried to reassure her, but the woman practically galloped into a run.

Dear God, now she was scaring the public with her obsession to catch even a tiny glimpse of Vic. What the hell was she doing? She was acting irrational, like a fucking stalker, for crying out loud. It was sick, and pathetic, yet she didn't give a damn. She needed her "Vic fix" before she could even dare think about writing. It'd become her infatuation, to see that face and that hard body.

Any hint of a glimpse sent her mind into work mode, helped her paint the silhouette of her characters into living, vibrant colors, helped her keep her guilt alive. The very guilt that had hooked its talons in her conscience the second she opened her package from the publisher and held *Vapor* in her hands. The cover had been even more amazing in her grasp than the copy saved as her background on her computer. Yet, running her hands over the glossiness brought back the striking colors of reality—the reality this book was written about.

She needed that guilt daily, needed a constant reminder of how utterly stupid she'd been to take something so fragile and beautiful, and then shatter it the way she'd done in the folds of the pages.

Her own reasons weren't good enough—that she couldn't escape the need to write what that night had created. It had brought her writing soul alive. Not to mention it'd been the hottest, most impulsive sex she'd ever had. She'd wanted to capture every detail, every vivid scene, and she had, in *Vapor*. That night had yanked her out of the closet and into the limelight of erotic inducements. It'd startled a novel from her mind. Without that night, her manuscripts would still be taking up valued space on her hard drive. Without that night, *Vapor* would have never been born. Or *Phantom*, or the rest following close behind it. It would have never given her the guts to click that send button, or the courage to let go of the characters she was clinging to like her very life depended on it.

Now, even with four contracts under her belt, with more proposals pending with the publisher, it still meant nothing. She'd used Vic, or rather, their incredible night, to boost her career.

She was a worthless excuse for a human being, and an even sorrier excuse for an author. She didn't deserve any fame if it meant Vic would never forgive her, or that she'd caused her any pain.

When movement in the restaurant caught her attention, Ashley straightened, straining for a view of the woman she couldn't wrestle from her mind, the woman she desperately wanted to find the courage to face again.

Instead, a waiter adjusted the blinds to block the setting sun from his customers, shutting out any hope of seeing Vic today.

With her head hung, Ashley made her way back to the car and drove home slowly, mentally bashing herself for not calling Vic, or at least e-mailing her. Some kind of apology was better than nothing at all. And all this spying from across the street wasn't getting her anywhere either. If anything, it was only making her crave every peek she could steal of Vic while making her rounds to chat with the customers, something Ashley had witnessed on several scouting trips before today. She was gorgeous. And she was gone.

Ashley needed to get her shit together. Her new career might very well depend on it. She snarled with the thought. Her career had been dying a slow and agonizing death from the second she held her creation in her hands. Luckily, she wrote *Phantom* on the tails of the first. God knew the following two she'd had to pry from her closing mind.

Vic deserved to hear those well-rehearsed words of apology in person. An e-mail or voicemail wouldn't do. If it was the last thing she did, she'd have to find the courage to step across the street, walk inside, and demand two minutes of her time.

After preparing a ready-made pasta packet, Ashley curled up on the couch with her laptop, only to stare at the computer screen, at the blinking curser sitting like an eerie specter in the middle of her blank document.

For months, she'd been unable to write a damn word, let alone a page. Her sexual crime nipped at her mind, building up that ugly brick wall each and every time she opened her laptop. The black hole, or mental block, well known to authors, stopped her dead in her tracks when it came to writing. Having to force herself to write the saggy middle paled in comparison to this particular brick wall, a brick wall she was sure wouldn't crumble until she'd made amends to Vic.

With a sigh, Ashley forked pasta into her mouth and concentrated on her newest novel. Well, the hopes of a new novel, anyway. She'd struggled to plot out the story, or rather the characters wouldn't stop clattering in her head long enough to figure out who and what they wanted to be. Seemed every character had Vic's eyes, her smile, and her gorgeous color-blocked hair.

"Fuck!" Ashley shoved the laptop away.

It seemed useless to bother writing anything, like trying to turn around on a narrow one-way street in a stretch limousine. Sooner or later her editor was going to demand that she change the appearance of her characters, or at the very least come up with a new color of eyes, or a new texture of hair, or God forbid, anything other than a crooked, dimpled smile. And that would destroy the whole concept of her story. Pretty soon the woman was going to demand that Ashley write anything at all. Right now, there wasn't a damn thing flowing across her monitor.

If she didn't find a way out of this funk, her new career was going to die a slow and painful death. Probably exactly what she deserved.

Hell, she knew that's exactly what she deserved.

The phone shrilled from beside her. She considered ignoring it but could use the sound of anyone's voice, including the flipping telemarketers.

She jerked the handset up and hit the talk button. "Hello."

"Let me guess, you're curled up on the couch with the laptop, bowl of boring pasta in your hand, or hold up, maybe you were daring tonight and popped a TV dinner into the microwave. Did I win a cookie?" Her best friend and super hot vampire erotica author, Caprice, cooed. The added bonus was she had two of the cutest and coolest kids Ashley had ever met, and a sexy husband who was never jealous of his wife's "lesbo" friend.

Ashley glanced at the pasta sitting like a congealed slop in her bowl, and her hunger vanished. She set the bowl on the coffee table. "Bitch."

Caprice laughed. "I've got big plans for you."

"Oh really? Let *me* guess, you want to drag me off to some book signing so I can set up all those fuck almighty books you keep spitting out of that brain of yours like chewing tobacco from a farmer's mouth. Wait, I'm not done. Then, like a good little work horse, you want me to conceal myself into the darkest corner out of sight while you paste your John Hancock into your huge compilation of books for your streaming line of adoring fans." She paused when Caprice didn't respond. "A few more books and you'll be caught up with your hero icon, AK. By the way, I won the whole fucking batch of cookies, didn't I?"

"Bitch. And first of all, I'll never be an Angela Knight, no matter how hard I try. She's in a league all her own. Second, no, as a matter of fact, you're wrong this time. Ha!"

Ashley considered any other options, but couldn't come up with a single thing. "You mean I actually get to sign the books for you? I get to be Caprice Hawke even for a few hours?" She joked and yearned for another book signing, for another view of Vic watching her from the back of the store.

Ashley pushed that image out of mind to focus on Caprice and whatever had made her giddy tonight.

She was so damn proud of her best friend. After years of tormenting herself as a personal aerobics instructor, Caprice finally quit her day job to become a full-time mother, along with the titles she'd given herself—chef, maid, and whore service. Ashley was positive the latter she welcomed with a smile when she crawled across that sexy husband of hers every night. The freedom of being a housewife opened a portal in her mind, and soon a writer was born. And from there, a best-selling author climbed from her shell, and multiple releases later, Caprice became a prized icon in the vampire world. Her copies disappeared from the shelves normally within weeks. Of course, her characters were straight, but that never kept the sex scenes from peaking Ashley's adrenaline. Caprice had a way of making her forget she was a lesbian while mentally begging some vampire to bite the shit out of her.

It also helped that Caprice had given her endless insight about the writing world, critiqued her sloppy chapters, run-ons and fragments included, without once trying to change her voice, and always gave her criticism Ashley sometimes didn't like. Every blood mark she splattered on Ashley's pages only made her skin thicker, and made her a better writer. Well, once, it did.

"You'd rather play *me* and give up meeting some hot chicks? I think not."

Ashley growled, hating the reminder that she was alone, that she could use some sexual release right about now. Her thoughts automatically drifted toward Vic and she struggled to push them away. "There's nothing better than being your lackey for two whole hours. But now my curiosity is piqued. Do tell. This has got to be something special."

"You're going to the charity ball in two weeks in my place."

"The masked ball? With those uppity, nose to the sky, rich asses, all dancing to some boring number in ball gowns that cost more than my damn house. I think not! Those precious kids have warped that sinfully sexy mind of yours. Do you know what number you just dialed?"

"Hmmm. This is Ashley Vaughn, right? The one sitting at this very second in her blue striped pajama pants with a hole ripped out of the left pants leg, the very one she got caught on the nail she keeps forgetting to hammer in on her back porch. The very one who just slid a bowl of pasta onto the coffee table, and the one who has a blank document open on her laptop, which, um, let me guess, is still sitting on the couch where you pushed it when that brick wall jumped up once again."

Ashley looked down at the laptop, at the arrow looking lonely as hell against the white screen. "I'm pathetic, aren't I?"

"Pathetic? Hmmm, let me think. Uh, yeah!"

"Thanks, friend." Ashley pushed off the couch and walked to the window to look out over the front yard. Across the street, children played hide-and-seek in their yard, the darkening sky assisting in their efforts at evasion.

She smiled when a little boy darted from behind a bush, ran to the driveway, dropped to the pavement, and scooted on his stomach under a minivan, his gaze searching for his assailant. Often, she wondered why she'd never wanted kids. Wasn't it supposed to be every woman's dream to spawn little mirror images of themselves?

Not that it mattered. Ashley had no intention of being a mother. Being an aunt to Caprice's rowdy boys was more than good enough for her. Did Vic want kids? And why the hell did it matter?

"Hey, what are friends for?" Caprice said.

"Well, for starters, not for forcing them to go to some damned masked ball, that's for sure. And why can't you go?"

"Got a last minute book signing. The bookstore had an author pull out suddenly. And speak of the devil, Angela fucking Knight is going to be there the same day. Can you friggin' imagine the crowd that'll be pushing the guts out of the bookstore, all those vampire lovers eagerly praying to sniff her panties?"

"You're heartless, that's what you are! I can be your bookie, hunchback slave, whatever you need for the day; it's fucking AK in the flesh, damn it. Take me with you, I beg you!"

"Okay. You can go."

"Really? I can go with you?"

"You bet. Flight leaves at five that morning."

Ashley could hear Caprice withholding as much of her snicker as possible, knowing full well she was deathly afraid of airplanes. A cold shiver snaked along her nerves as she imagined looking down over white puffy clouds, the plane descending at incredible speeds, nose-first toward the ground beneath.

"I hope your tampon leaks in front of your entire fan club. Or that you have a huge green booger in your nose without a tissue in sight."

Caprice burst out laughing. "Talk about heartless, sheesh. But seriously, all I need you to do is show up."

"I'm not doing it."

"Pleeeeese," Caprice begged.

"No."

"I'll love and adore you forever."

"You already do."

"I'll send Dan over to give you a lap dance."

Ashley grinned. "You'd hook out your very own hubby? Must be pretty important. What's the catch?"

"No catch. Well, maybe one."

"And that is what?"

"To show up."

Ashley knew better than that. "That's it?"

"And sign your name on the guest list in my place."

"And?" Ashley could hear another unspoken "and" in the air.

"Um, be present during the auction?"

"Caprice!"

"You just have to stand there...swear!"

Ashley huffed. "You're killing me. What else?"

"And...dance with the winner, male or female."

Ashley swung away from the window. "Hell no. That's it. I refuse!"

Caprice's laughter rattled through the phone and Ashley knew she'd been suckered. "Bitch."

"You're too easy." Caprice composed herself. "So you'll do it?"

"For you, but you're gonna owe me big time, starting with Dan grinding that six-pack in my face. Besides, what the hell else do I have to do besides stare at these bland walls willing my fingers to type?"

"Stellar! I knew I could count on you 'cause you're a super trouper like that."

Ashley gave a grunt. Caprice was right. Ashley was a sucker for her. "Fine, but I'm leaving as soon as I throw your book at the winner."

"Mean ass! And you can't leave then. The fun is in the adjacent ballroom. Maybe you can hook up with some stranger and have hot, unadulterated sex."

Ashley imagined the scene of rich women, glitzy diamonds sparkling from their fingers. She shook her head, positive a charity ball wouldn't hold anything to make her yearn for sex.

Ashley walked back to the couch and fell into the cushions. "My writer's block is getting worse. I can't fucking take this anymore."

"Write something, anything. Even if you have to write what's going on in your mind. Don't stop writing until there's nothing left."

"I tried that," Ashley lied. When her fingers hovered over the keys, all she saw was Vic, and then she couldn't write a thing.

"Then you didn't write everything. Write about your evening with your mystery woman."

Ashley rolled her eyes. Hadn't writing about that particular night gotten her into this mess to begin with? She had a beautiful cover to prove that she'd used Vic in an awful way, though she'd never in a million years meant for it to be like that. Their night had been earth shattering. Their night had opened her portal to what she prayed would be a top hit.

She hung her head. Vic would never see it any other way. She would never see that Ashley had never meant to use her, that the book was her way of holding that night close to her heart for eternity, and she'd shared her sacred experience with every lesbian who opened the binding.

"And I don't mean expanding it into another novel. Write how you felt about it, how it affected you. And for the last fucking time, every author in the world writes truth into their stories. It's called hands-on research. You haven't done anything illegal by writing something that happened to you personally."

"That's bullshit, and you know it."

"Okay, so you went a little overboard, maybe could have altered a few of those facts, but it's still life, Ash. We're all guilty of taking our experiences and pasting them onto the pages. Stop beating yourself up over it. Or go fucking find her and tell her you're sorry. Maybe then your wall will come crumbling down."

Ashley turned toward the computer. She couldn't dare tell Caprice she was Vic's stalker, that she watched from a tiny alcove across the street for a smidgen of a peek. Caprice would commit her.

Maybe a tiny e-mail would end this fatigue, would end this endless writer's block once and for all. It was a cheap shot, but better than sitting here living with so much guilt.

"As for your book signing, since I've been manhandled to do your dirty work, I better get the newest release autographed by Ms. AK. It should read, 'To Ashley, the hottest lesbian erotic writer I've ever known. I bow to you.'"

Caprice grumbled. "You're a pain in the ass. Anyone ever told you that?"

"You…like, a hundred times. Now, go give those awesome boys a kiss from their aunt Ashley. And tell Dan, my all time favorite, sexy handyman, that my faucet is leaking again."

"Can't kiss the boys, they're zombies right now in front of the Wii. If I touch them, they crash back to Earth, and it's peaceful around the house when they're aliens in outer space." Caprice chuckled. "But I'll send Dan over tomorrow to fix that damn leak again. I swear, I think you break things on purpose just to stare at his ass."

"I do." Ashley blew a kiss into the phone then hung up.

She stared for more agonizing minutes at the blank page. Nothing would come. Not even a word of what her characters were doing, what they were thinking, or even where they might be having sex. With a grumble, she finally opened the manager file in her Web site and inserted the date and time of the masked ball into her agenda calendar. She surfed the charity ball Web site and found a flyer so she pasted that onto the page as well.

With a huff, she brought the new document back up and then tapped a staccato rhythm with her fingernails, begging the gods to make the story flow.

Fuck almighty, she needed an end to this torture. She needed closure.

She needed Vic.

Chapter Nine

Vic held the door open for a couple entering the little mom-and-pop sandwich shop. A little girl with stick-straight blond hair and striking green eyes bounced around their legs squealing something about chicken fingers and soda. Once the trio was safely out of the way, and Heather had stepped through the door, Vic fell in behind her.

She automatically stuffed her hands in her jeans pocket as they began their lazy stroll down the outdoor strip mall.

"What's got you so bummed, pouty face? You've barely spoken all night." Heather reached out and took Vic's hand from her pocket. She smiled up at Vic as she snuggled against her side. "Wasn't your Italian hoagie any good? That's normally your favorite."

Vic squeezed her hand, thankful Heather was here with her tonight. She'd needed a night out to get her mind off her life, her job, and Ashley fucking Vaughn. And she needed a late-night fuck as well. Friends with benefits always came in handy in a pinch.

Heather looked good enough to swallow in her flower print sundress, hair the color of spun gold nestled in a messy bun at the nape of her neck, and those daring deep blue eyes telling Vic all she needed to know, that she wanted the same as Vic.

She needed Heather tonight, needed their bodies grinding against each other, sweating, and releasing pent-up tension. Her day hadn't gone well, starting with a screw-up with the meat order that was certainly her fault, and ending disastrously when three waiters called in sick, as well as one of her chefs. Not that she was opposed to throwing on her apron and diving into the grill. Quite the opposite, actually. Being in the kitchen with the hustle and bustle, shouting orders above the ruckus, and sliding filled plates down the counter—it all reminded her of where she'd been, and how far she'd come to make an honest name for herself. But lately, she just couldn't think coherently, and it showed in her work after a second attempt not to burn salmon, of all things, her all-time specialty.

She'd finally admitted defeat when a dish slipped out of her hands, scattering her last attempt at an edible meal onto the tiled floor. Emanuel, her top chef, had shooed her out of the kitchen, mumbling God knew what in Spanish. Only when he was flustered, and had enough of the tension, would he use his natural-born language. She knew then it was time to call it a night, and seek refuge in Heather's arms.

Come to think of it, how long had it been? Weeks? Months? She knew the answer. Since a fucking "in the flesh" plot seeker had brought her to her knees with her life splattered all over the pages of a crappy novel. Okay, so it wasn't crap. God, it was fucking hot as sin to reread their entire night through Ashley's eyes. But that wasn't the point. The point was, it was downright despicable how she used women for a plot.

Vic shook her head. Fuck, what was wrong with her anymore? How could she let that bitch affect her like this? She couldn't even do what she loved most—cook. And worse, it wasn't only affecting her work, it was affecting everything else in her life as well. Her sleep, her eating habits, and her sex life. Not that she had much of one, but she could always count on Heather to give her what her body craved.

She gave Heather a reassuring smile. The last thing she needed was Heather giving her a pity fuck, even though that's probably what it boiled down to, a fact she wouldn't share with Heather. "The sandwich was delish. I think I'm just tired after that hellacious day at work."

Heather waved her hand in dismissal. "All rubbish, my dear butch. Tomorrow will be another day, and even if you fuck that one up, believe it or not, another one comes shortly after that. Gives you another chance to fuck that one up, too." She chucked Vic in the arm. "Chin up, girlie. Make a better tomorrow. And stop all that whining. For crying out loud, you sound like my five-year-old nephew pouting over his damn broken iPod. And who the fuck gives their five-year-old a freaking iPod?"

Vic shrugged, inexperienced in the tactics of parents' reasons to spoil their children. She'd never wanted children, still didn't. She did good to keep up with her niece, all eleven years of her. How her sister Karen was still sane after living with such a wild child, she'd never know. She often snickered over her ranting on their monthly luncheons. The old saying had to be true—like mother, like daughter. God knew Karen had been far worse than Gabby could ever dream of being at that age. Vic was living testimony to her sporadic tantrums when their parents didn't give Karen her way, God rest their loving souls. She was sure they'd have spoiled their granddaughter beyond rotten, or her mother, rather, who outlived her father by ten plus years before colon cancer took her life…the exact cancer to take her father. They'd died before she got a chance to prove their desire for gourmet cooking ran deep in her veins.

Heather huffed. "It's a downright shame what kids can finagle out of their parents these days. At his age, I was already doing chores. God forbid there be a reward in the mix."

Vic smiled. She'd been blessed with loving parents who rewarded good behavior and ignored the bad, save for those hard, glaring eyes that dared her or Karen to continue their misbehavior. For the most part, she and her sister turned out okay. Well, minus the fact that she'd never been trained in how to deal with a bruised ego, or a damaged heart, if there were such training.

Seemed Ashley was dominating every aspect of her life, starting with their glorious night, then ending with that monstrosity of a book, making a fucking mockery of that night, all in black and white for all the world to see. She'd read the whole book, not once, but three times. The bitch had some fucking nerve, no matter how hot the pages were. Every little detail of their time together lay bare. Why hadn't Ashley gone the whole hog and named the restaurant— at least it would've given it some free publicity—or hell, even given her address and cell phone number so every lesbian this side of the hemisphere could help her forget she'd ever laid eyes on the queen bitch.

Vic's anger wouldn't set her free, wouldn't give her a moment's peace. Worse, she couldn't tell a living soul, not even Heather. Sure, Heather could fuck her tonight and then lend her a friendly shoulder tomorrow, but there were some things best kept private. She felt safer with those secrets harbored inside her head. Actually, she wasn't sure anyone would dare believe how stupid and naïve she'd been to fall into Ashley's baited trap, even Heather.

She almost laughed at the thought. Heather would have a ball with such a juicy tidbit. She'd wear her fingers out texting that information to the entire lesbian Web ring before Vic could get halfway through the part about dinner.

Regardless of Heather's inability to keep a secret, their sex was amazing, their friendship even more amazing. Vic was sometimes bummed that that was all there was to them—only friends with benefits. Besides, Heather wasn't the secret-sharing friend that Vic needed right now. Right now, she needed her sex partner. Right now, she wanted an orgasm ripped from her body, and Heather was just the person to get that job done, no strings attached.

"Hey, you wanna come with me to the art museum tomorrow? I promised Nikki I'd go take a peek at her new piece." Heather leaned in, lowering her voice into a sexy whisper. "You and I would have to part ways soon after, however. She promised me some breathless sex. I couldn't turn her down." She winked. "She's so good in the sack, can't help myself."

Vic smiled, not even a twinge of jealousy eating at her. "Better than sitting around my office staring at order forms. I'm game."

"Have you changed your mind about the masked ball?"

Vic grunted. "I'm not going to some lame masked ball. You can totally forget that!"

"Oh come on, you pussy. It might be fun for you. Might even find some mysterious chick to fuck." Heather waggled her brow. "Could be hot for you."

Vic shook her head. "If I wanted to fuck a masked stranger I'd go to the damn BDSM club uptown."

Heather stopped dead in her tracks, jerking Vic back with the sudden halt. "I'll take you there, right after the masked ball. Oh, wait, it'll have to be the next day. I have sexual plans right after the ball as well." She winked and started walking again. "But seriously, say the word and you'll be underground and hogtied to a torture tower."

"A what?"

Heather waved away the question. "You'd have to see it to believe it. Speaking of which, I could use a good lashing...been a while."

Vic chuckled, wondering what else there was about Heather she might never know. "You're a pistol. And no, I'm not going to any of the above."

Heather huffed. "Chickenshit."

"Slut."

"Yeah, and your point?" Heather veered them toward the bookstore while Vic grinned. God how she needed Heather tonight. "Let's go check out the new releases. Maybe I'll be in luck and find a new lesbian title. Lord knows I've read everything King and Koontz have put out." She gave a slight stomp as she turned toward the store. "I need to read hot, lesbian sex. No more horror books!"

Vic hadn't entered the bookstore since the day she bought *Vapor*, the biggest slap in the face she'd ever experienced. The place only made her growl, made her think of things she'd rather forget. Things she couldn't fucking forget.

She allowed Heather to lead her inside then shook her head as Heather bee-lined for the naughty corner. She slowed at the cookbook section to scan any new titles then smirked at all the horrendous displays on the covers.

Maybe she ought to consider putting together a compilation of her favorite recipes and publish her own cookbook. From the pitiful selection here, it was sure to be a hit. Better still, she could stick the very dish Ashley had eaten on the front cover with a tagline, "Eaten by Ashley Vaughn…oh, and this dish was too." Vic smothered a sardonic laugh.

The bitch!

When Heather let out a piercing squeal from behind her, Vic spun around to find herself face-to-face with a human-size poster of Ashley Vaughn. Her breath caught and hung like a thick fog and a lump lodged itself tight in her throat.

Her gaze drifted down the oversize cardboard to the words announcing her forthcoming release, *Phantom*.

Heather jumped up and down like a giddy teenager. "I'm going to come in my thong. I swear I am." Heather kissed the lips of the poster then placed it back on the floor. "Dear God, she writes the hottest sex I've ever laid eyes on. I masturbate to almost every one…can't help myself. They're so sizzling."

Vic wanted to tell her to lower her voice, that there could be children within earshot, but she couldn't tear herself away from those stilled amber eyes. Her mind whiplashed her back in time, to Ashley bucking against her face on the staircase, to the sounds of her coming hard around Vic's tongue. Even now, the sounds ripped at her soul, tore at her heart with hot, metal talons.

When physical pain seared her crotch, she forced her gaze away from Ashley's smiling face. The bitch had used her for the sake of her career. She was nothing more than a plot whore.

Heather cleared her throat and Vic blinked out of her trance. "You look like you saw a ghost, or maybe that's a look of 'I want to fuck that smile right off her face.'" She looked from the poster back to Vic. "I'd sure do her before she could ask my name."

"You do most everyone before they can ask your name." Vic smiled playfully.

Heather scoffed and then nodded in agreement, her smile bright against her red lips. "No need to waste time on such nonsense as names, right?" She winked then dived back into the lesbian section.

Vic turned back to the cookbooks, seething. Ashley's career was definitely taking off, all starting by pasting the truth into fiction.

The witch! How could she fucking do that? Sure, the characters' names had changed, as well as Vic's occupation, but the rest was their night, right down to the NASCAR getaway she did leaving Vic's house.

"Guess I'll have to wait until *Phantom* comes out to read any kind of decent sex." Heather wedged up against Vic and displayed her selection of vampire books by an author named Angela Knight.

The name sparked a cord of memory, of Ashley telling her she was "...*only the hottest erotic vampire writer ever known to mankind. Aside from my best friend, that is.*"

"In the meantime, these will have to quench my thirst. I'm kind of into all that neck-biting sex, even though the characters are straight as arrows. Good thing for her she writes hot-ass alphas... most of whom I can imagine as butch." She looked up at Vic and hissed between clenched teeth. "Bite me, baby."

Vic scooted her to the checkout before she did just that.

What had she done so terrible to make Ashley use their sacred night the way she had? Had the sly bitch written *Phantom* the same way? God rest the poor bastard when she laid eyes on every last detail of their sexual encounter bound in a pretty cover.

Jealousy, slow and hot, like thick lava creeping from a porous cavern, slithered through her gut. She almost reeled back from the emotion. *Are you fucking kidding me? I get jealous now, after the bitch ruined me in the most monstrous way possible. Fuck, am I a pussy or what? Or just pussy whipped?*

Vic almost hung her head in shame, disgusted with herself for still wanting Ashley. Heather paid her tab while Vic fumed.

Suddenly, she couldn't get out of the store fast enough, couldn't fuck Heather quickly enough. She needed to forget, needed to feel something other than the strums of her personal vibrator tonight, or the hurt echoing through her heart.

As soon as they stepped out onto the sidewalk, Vic pulled Heather against her chest and kissed her. She didn't care who saw her and didn't care what they thought if they did.

Heather reacted to the kiss by palming her hand around the

nape of Vic's neck and deepening the connection. Vic wished that kiss meant something. It didn't. Their kisses weren't like those of a couple in love but merely two women who found solace and great sex in each other's arms.

What she wouldn't give to find someone who made her heart jolt at the sound of her voice, to be reckless to get home to her every day of her life.

Heather wasn't that person. But right now, Heather could make her thoughts cease, could make her body twitch with anticipation, just like it was doing right now.

Vic pulled away. "Can I offer you some hot sex for our nightly conclusion?"

"Hell yes, you can. You always do, don't you?" Heather tapped Vic's bottom lip. "I'll race you."

Twenty minutes later, Vic pulled into her driveway to find Heather already waiting on the patio. She smiled, hopeful that a night of rough sex would put an end to her stream of bad days, and please, God, just a few hours with her mind void of anything to do with Ashley Vaughn.

As soon as she closed and locked the door behind them, Heather was clinging to her, her tongue soft as it crept inside Vic's mouth.

Vic groped at her ass, pulling her thighs up and around her hips. On steady legs, she wound her way up the staircase, stalling in the spot where she'd laid Ashley down. Would Heather make the same sounds? Would she bring Vic's temperature past the boiling point with the slight bucking of her hips?

Either way, she couldn't bring herself to lay Heather down. That spot was sacred. And sentimental.

With Heather grinding those lean hips, Vic climbed the remaining steps, stumbled into the bedroom, and landed on top of her in the middle of the bed.

Robotically, they undressed each other, familiar hands caressing one another, until they were naked against the comforter.

"You're strange tonight." Heather rolled Vic onto her back and slid down between her thighs, positioning herself in the alcove.

"Strange in a good way, or strange in a creepy-crawly kind of way?" Vic widened her legs, hands already forming a fist in Heather's thick mane.

Heather ran her tongue along Vic's slit and all thoughts slammed to the back of her mind. She always had a way of making Vic numb.

"In a weird, freaky way. I think I like you better in your normal take-charge mode." Heather drew on her clit and Vic arched automatically.

"Mmmm, I'm liking you better in that role right now." Vic gripped her fingers tightly, pulling Heather snugger against her pussy. "Take charge, baby."

A single finger entered her, followed soon by another, thrusting slow on the in stroke, faster on the out stroke, until Vic was pumping against the mattress.

She screwed her eyes tight, and fuck if Ashley wasn't there, those damned amber eyes making love to her…fucking her all over again.

With a start, she opened her eyes. Ashley didn't deserve to be in her mind, or in her thoughts.

Vic leaned forward and pulled Heather from between her legs, up, until she was straddling her thighs. Slowly, she started grinding upward, circling her pelvic bone against Heather's pussy.

"I want to watch you come." Vic palmed her hips and drove against her.

What she really wanted was a face to replace the one determined to invade her mind. She wanted Ashley out of her fucking thoughts, out of her fucking head.

Heather started circling slowly, pressing her pussy against Vic's pelvic bone. Harder, faster, stronger, Heather ground herself against Vic. She palmed her breasts and pinched her nipples, all while Vic watched her, shoving Ashley's face clear from her mind.

When Heather sucked in air and slung her head back, Vic rolled her onto her back and drove two fingers inside her, hovering over her, watching her, instilling that face in her mind.

She knew tonight would be the last night she ever fucked her best friend. Even familiar sex couldn't shove that conniving vixen from her mind.

Long after Heather had shown herself out, Vic still lay on the bed staring at the ceiling. Sleep was a myth, had been for months With a huff, she slung the flimsy sheet off, pulled on a T-shirt and jeans, and padded into the computer room adjacent to the bedroom.

The motherboard hummed to life while she waited. Since sleep was determined not to engulf her, she could at least get next week's food order taken care of, as well as the payroll. Anything other than laying there thinking, wondering…and hating.

It only took a few minutes to line up the order forms and then enter the hours for the payroll, and then she was back to twiddling her thumbs. She started surfing the Web, checking out Olivia's cruise line for any eye-catching vacation getaways, and finally she huffed when she found herself checking the week's weather forecast. How pathetic could she get?

She closed every window and stared at the screensaver of cobblestone sidewalks weaving along a narrow one-way street of Provincetown, Massachusetts. It was a place she'd always wanted to visit, but never had anyone who stayed long enough in her life to take there. Or rather, work was always too pressing to leave.

According to friends who'd been there, you could walk freely down the streets hand-in-hand with your partner, male or female, mixing and mingling with gay or straight. She wanted to go there, wanted to snuggle with someone she loved on the beach and share a romantic candlelight dinner before enjoying a night of incredible sex accompanied by the sound of ocean waves crashing onto the shore.

Almost subconsciously, Vic opened a new browser page, and double-clicked Ashley's Web site icon.

The newest cover, *Phantom*, dominated the home page with a release date a few months ahead. It was one book she definitely wouldn't read. Some poor soul would be crying her eyes out with that release. She was better off not reading the details of Ashley's next victim.

She clicked the blog icon, but only skimmed over the contents, then went to the news page. One day, she knew this page would announce another book signing. She feared that day, feared what she might do, or not do, when that day came. She envisioned what she'd say face-to-face with Ashley. Would she be brave and approach her, or remain her cool and calm self and just watch her from the backdrop of the room, just like she had the first time she met her? Maybe just a dark glare would put fear in her throughout her reading. The thought gave Vic hope.

Thankfully, the page didn't announce a book signing where Vic might be tempted to arrive, though what it did say was worse.

STEP INTO YOUR SHINY TUX AND GLAMOROUS BALL GOWNS, THEN HIDE BEHIND A MASK OF YOUR CHOICE. TONIGHT IS YOUR NIGHT TO SLIP OUT OF YOUR BORING LIVES AND INTO A WORLD OF MYSTERY, WHERE ANYTHING IS POSSIBLE.

THE HILTON WILL HOST ITS 25TH ANNUAL CHARITY EVENT ON FRIDAY AT 7 P.M. AUCTION BEGINS AT 6 P.M.

JOIN ONE, OR THE OTHER, OR BOTH, BUT PLEASE EMPTY THOSE WALLETS AT THE DOOR. DONATIONS ARE A MUST.

IN ATTENDANCE:
    MANNING POWERS
    STARLA KEYS
    ASHLEY VAUGHN IN ATTENDANCE FOR CAPRICE HAWKE
    DALIA CRAIG
    ...AND A FEW OTHER SURPRISE VISITORS.

LEAVE YOUR FEAR AT HOME. BRING YOUR COURAGE TO THE DANCE FLOOR.

COME ONE. COME ALL

Vic leaned back in her chair, a smile twitching on her lips.

Seemed she'd have to reconsider her stance on this event. Payback time!

"So, we meet again, Ms. Ashley Vaughn…you fucking plot whore!"

CHAPTER TEN

Ashley moved through the crowded ballroom, feeling like a wisp of white satin in her new designer dress against the men in their starched black tuxedos and the women in their bright, glamorous gowns.

She'd squared away her obligations of being in this dreadful place tonight, had signed the guest log in place of Caprice, tapped her feet impatiently while Caprice's month-old release went to the highest bidder, and just as she was ready to escape the confined hotel lobby, she heard hoorays bellowing from the adjacent ballroom.

Curiosity had gotten the better of her. An hour later, she was still cruising the room in hopes of something that might spike her attention, something that might give her hope for a plot. So far, nothing.

Four large crystal chandeliers hung above the polished wood dance floor with a disco ball displayed dead center. Sparks of light caught the glass droplets and shot a kaleidoscope of colors over the dancers, circling around the room in a blur of brilliant hues.

Three long tables took up the entire back wall laden with all manner of exotic finger foods and large crystal bowls with fountains of punch cascading into their depths. Along the east wall was a bar, the exact spot Ashley now wanted to park herself. Already well out of her element, she couldn't summon any enthusiasm for this lavish gala, even for Caprice. Staring at her laptop seemed far more interesting than watching the ritzy people waltz around the dance floor with their costume jewelry catching every hue of the rainbow.

Ashley saw a woman wedged against the entrance to the restrooms, her beau sucking at her neck like a hungry vampire, and she gulped.

Hiding her shock, Ashley turned away, scared she'd see way more than she bargained for. Or maybe she should continue to watch. It seemed they might be the most interesting couple in this boring place. She almost collided with another couple who seemed to be just as sex craved, their lips locked as they danced at the outer edge of the dance floor.

My God, what kind of charity ball is this, anyway?

Caprice had forgotten to mention the part about orgies, or public sex. Maybe that's why she'd insisted Ashley take her place only using the excuse of a book signing.

Ashley scooted around the oblivious couple and approached the bar. The bartender dragged his gaze away from another couple lip-locked at the far end of the counter. The expression he shot her announced he wasn't happy about her diverting his attention from the free show.

She ordered a rum and Coke then gave him the free token the hostess had given her when she signed the guest list, which he tossed into a basket before mixing her drink. He slammed it on the counter and turned away from her in complete dismissal, his sights weaving over the crowd before landing on the couple now very close to needing a room. Thank goodness they were on the ground floor of a hotel. Lord knew they were going to need a bed soon.

Fuck, is everyone in this place high on some new sex drug?

She looked down at her glass, half expecting to see white foam dissolving in the center. There wasn't.

With as much grace as she could muster, she wove her way back through the crowd, noticing more couples along her path, all of whom seemed to be in some state of sexual fog, hands groping, mouths sealed. Maybe she should have been drinking with this crowd instead of listening to the tedious numbers from the auctioneer. Seemed some were having the time of their lives.

A couple bumped into Ashley, almost making her spill her drink.

She scowled as they skirted around her, parting the crowd like a bow wave as they rushed toward the exit.

With a grunt, she found an empty table, sat down, and crossed her legs. One drink and she'd be on her way. She came, she saw, and she watched. Wasn't the fact that she turned up good enough to please Caprice?

The sheer tattered strips of her white satin dress slipped off her knees, revealing her legs clad in white stockings. She arched her foot in the air, rotating her ankle, loving the snug fit of the white-ribbon stilettos climbing her legs, crossing over her shins, tied in a single delicate knot at her lower calf.

For the first time in a very long time, she actually felt sexy in a dress. She made a mental note to remember the exact way the material caressed her skin, the way it revealed a tantalizing peek of her upper thighs as she moved her legs. Maybe, with a lot of luck and steady concentration, she could find a way to get the words flowing on her computer, maybe she could find a way to shove Vic to the back of her mind long enough to write just one fucking paragraph.

Her readers depended on her to bring the words to life, to add color to the otherwise blank pages of her creations.

She begged the heavens above that tonight she might find a creative space in her mind with enough room to whip up some kind of coherent chapters.

With a sigh, she let her leg fall back over the other, and glanced around the crowded room. She asked herself once again what she was really doing here. For Caprice…yes, that was it. So Caprice could go rub elbows with the fucking queen of vampire erotica, her motivator and hero, Angela fucking Knight. What she wouldn't give to be with them right now.

Couples snuggled as they drifted lazily to a slow song. Was it possible that some of them had actually met for the first time tonight, that someone here would actually meet their soul mate? Rarely did anyone meet their knight in shining armor in surroundings like these. Or, in her case, a warrior princess in tight fitting jeans, or a tux, since jeans were banned from this particular event.

Not that she was looking for Ms. Right. She'd already met her, fucked her, and then ran like the coward she was. That story was a closed book now, literally. As soon as she could apologize to Vic, make the amends she knew she had to make, she could cut those last strings and walk away, finally be free of the guilt plaguing her daily.

Ashley sipped her drink and watched as women and men broke into a waltz when the music changed. The strobe lights caught their gems and sequins, making darts of color pierce the air around them. With a sigh, she let her gaze cast out over their heads, studying the many different styles that must have taken hours to set. She attempted to describe one in particular; wave after wave of blond hair with black highlights, rode the back of her head, yet the front was laid over like a toupee. Ashley shook her head. Why in the world anyone would pay high-dollar prices for such a do she'd never know. That particular hairstyle would never make it to her pages.

She mentally rolled her eyes. What fucking pages?

All she wanted right now was to get the hell out of Dodge and back to the unfinished, or rather, not yet begun chapter of her newest book. Her editor would be tapping her e-mail very soon to remind her that a deadline fast approached. Hopefully, she'd gathered enough details from her short visit to get the juices flowing.

Fuck, who was she kidding? As soon as she curled up with the laptop that fucking brick wall would immediately spring up from nowhere and block her vision. What was it going to take to tear it down, brick by brick if she had to?

Vic. Damn it. Vic was her only option and she knew it.

She desperately missed the thrill of writing, the rush that it gave her with every tale she created. The characters left her breathless as she unfolded their lives. She carried them through their conflicts and black moments, to their peaks and fireworks, and now, of course, their happily ever after climax.

This ballroom filled with swishing, colorful gowns and starch-stiff tuxedos wasn't giving her a damn thing, not a single spark of interest for a new plotline. She might as well be at home staring at a blank document.

Piercing laughter caught her attention and she turned to find a butch in a savvy tuxedo carrying a blonde toward the exit. Her attention spiked as she tagged them as a lesbian couple. So far, the entire room had seemed to consist of straight couples. She relaxed with a smile; family was around her. The woman's captive playfully kicked her black pumps in a fake attempt to escape. By the bright red smile on her radiant face, escaping was the last thing on her mind. And then they disappeared from sight, no doubt to one of the rooms upstairs where someone would be howling the other's name very soon.

Ashley gave a deep, longing sigh and leaned back, pushing her newly highlighted curls over her shoulder. Vic came to mind, as she always did when Ashley least expected her. That night had altered her life. The fire inside her had expunged her mushy romances, and erotic inducements had been born for the long haul. Of course, the erotic stories had already begun, all starting with her short story in the anthology, but Vic had pushed the door wide open. Hell, she'd ripped the hinges off the doorframe. Ashley's success had been born.

"Is this seat empty?" A male voice came from above and behind her.

She looked over her shoulder to find a set of deep blue eyes behind a black satin mask staring at her cleavage. She should have known the dress the sales clerk insisted would be stunning on her would bring out the vultures looking for free pussy. And here the vulture was now.

His dyed-dark hair parted on the side, a hint of a receding hairline visible, not her idea of sexy. The fact he was male made it even worse. She wasn't a man-hater, just a genuine woman lover.

"My eyes are up here, darling. And yes, the seat is empty." Ashley looked away. "If you sit in it, mine will be, too."

"Ah, we have a live one." The man chuckled. "You've been alone all night. Figured you could use some company."

"I'm alone for a reason." Ashley released an aggravated breath.

"You're not hitting on my date, are you?" A raspy feminine voice broke through the shroud of dull tunes filling the room.

Fire shot down Ashley's spine as the woman's voice sparked a cord of memory, of a raspy voice asking her to dinner from across a card table.

"Sorry. I didn't realize this beauty was with you." The man scooted away with a nod, cheeks pink with embarrassment.

As much as Ashley wanted to protest someone's claim on her, she was happy to have the man go away for any reason, and desperate to turn around to find mousse-colored eyes staring down at her.

She turned to see the culprit, and her heart plummeted.

There, in all her butch glory, stood Vic smiling down on her, a midnight blue mask hiding her eyebrows and cheeks.

Poisonous seduction oozed over her lean frame encased in a sexy tailored tux.

Desire shot through Ashley like a tornado.

Lord help her, she wanted to hike the tattered edges of her slinky dress up and wrap her legs around Vic's face, grind her hips until her orgasm shattered her guilt. She hadn't felt that spark of desire since Vic had laid her down on that staircase, since she fucked her against a tiled bathroom wall.

Why had she been scared so shitless of her emotions? Why had she run like a wimp? She struggled for the answers while Vic stood motionless, towering over her like an avenging angel.

Staring at Vic now, with half her face sheltered behind the mask, Ashley couldn't recall the emotions she'd run from. Had it been the control she'd found, or the fact that Vic had made her lose her own? Something had scared the wits out of her, but damn if she could find them now.

Did it really matter? That night had brought to life something new in her. Every sizzling erotic tale she wrote involved alpha females seducing strong-willed women who were determined to hang onto every last shard of control, just what the readers wanted. She owed that to Vic. Wickedly sad, every heroine lost her power sooner or later, their heroines sucking away their dominance in a single slurp. Once again, she owed those creations to Vic, or rather, the sinfully hot night embedded in her mind.

However, unlike her own tale, their endings always culminated with them in each other's arms, declaring undying love.

Ashley prayed Vic would say something, anything. She mentally banged her head for running away from things she didn't understand.

Would she be a fool to tell Vic she understood them now, or at least was open to understanding them?

Vic finally moved and eased onto the empty chair, snapping Ashley out of her trance. Her suave posture oozed with authority, making cream pool against Ashley's silk thong. Ashley cast that same manipulation of power into her characters, made them strong, and made them demand obedience.

Well, that was, until the muse slammed into a brick obstacle and self-destructed.

Vic slid her arm over the back of her chair and turned to look at Ashley. "Long time, no see. Can I get you another drink?"

Ashley's mind overflowed dangerously fast with all the things she'd rehearsed. Suddenly, she couldn't think of a fucking line, of a single word. If Vic was furious about the publication of *Vapor*, she was damn sure hiding it well. What were the chances she hadn't read it?

"I already have one, thanks." Ashley tried to drag her gaze away from those hypnotic eyes, mesmerized by their sparkle.

A Clorox smile greeted her. "How's life been?"

Miserable. Every day. Completely miserable. And I can't fucking write because of you. Because I may have hurt you. Because I can't stop thinking about your face buried between my thighs on a fuck almighty staircase.

"Life's been, well, good. I guess." *Fucking tell her how sorry you are. Tell her you needed to keep that night alive, that you needed a daily reminder of how stupid you are.*

"I'm glad to hear it." Vic turned away to look out over the dancers. "Congratulations, by the way."

And there it was…in her face long before Ashley was ready for it, and answering her curiosity if Vic had cracked open the book.

Hadn't she prepared herself for this very minute, for this exact face-off?

Ashley hung her head. Years' worth of training couldn't have prepared her for the emotions rushing through her body, at the heat nestling between her legs even as her heart drooped like a thirsty flower. "Vic, I'm—"

"Dance with me," Vic interrupted just as Ashley was finding her wits, and her courage.

Ashley looked up and found a wicked smile crawling across Vic's lips. She wanted to reach out and touch that smile, caress those sexy lips, slip her finger inside her luscious mouth to feel her wet tongue swirl against her skin in a soft suckle.

"Could we talk first?" Ashley's courage was growing by the second, spurred by Vic's strange aloofness.

Vic pushed out of the chair and grabbed Ashley by the arm. "Nothing to talk about, sexy." With more strength than Ashley wanted to be manhandled with at this moment, Vic led her toward the dance floor.

Ashley pulled back but Vic's fingers bit into her flesh. "Hey! You're hurting me." Against her body's common sense, her pussy throbbed sickly with need.

When Vic pulled her into the throng of grinding bodies, Ashley yanked her arm out of that steely grasp. She clenched her jaw tight as she met Vic's hard stare head-on. "What the hell is your problem?"

Vic only smiled and leaned in, her cinnamon breath feathering across Ashley's neck. "I thought you liked it rough."

Ashley gave her a blank stare as their bodies started swaying. Her crotch ached. For some perverted reason, her pussy sparked with fire, causing her to want to escape from the safe, boring life dictated by common sense. She wanted release from her guarded inhibitions. Worse, her pussy wept for satisfaction, for the way she knew Vic's body could satisfy her.

She allowed Vic to guide her, to lead her, to control her. Christ, she wasn't a woman so easily controlled, no matter how her body kept telling her otherwise. Sure, Vic had a way of making her jump into the fire, but hadn't she grown from that experience? Hadn't she learned a hard lesson from that single night?

The lights flickered and dimmed. A sensual beat of drums echoed around the room. The crowd of dancers swayed in a slow carnality with their partners.

Vic stopped and turned those brilliant eyes on her. Seriousness clouded her intense stare. "One more dance. Then you're free to leave."

Ashley wanted to tell her she was free to go right now, that no amount of vibrations in her pussy could stop her from fleeing, but her mind wouldn't let her mouth say the words, nor would her body let her move toward the exit.

She simply nodded and placed her hand in Vic's, liking the feel of her now gentle grasp, as well as the warmth slipping around the small of her back from Vic's free hand, pulling her closer.

Ashley closed her eyes and let Vic guide their sway. Could Vic feel the gripping sexual tension that was far stronger than the both of them?

The strum of slow guitars increased.

Vic's hand caressed the flesh of her back, daringly close to the cutout just above her ass, then followed the seam back up to her shoulders where the spaghetti strap curved over her shoulder.

Ashley relaxed against the soft trail of fingers, though she wanted nothing more than to guide them beneath her hem, to have them plunge into her slick pussy until an orgasm robbed her of coherency.

Coherent! She needed to be coherent to say what she had to say, not sexually drugged and unable to think straight. "Vic, I really need to—"

"You talk too much, Ashley." Vic ducked her face to Ashley's shoulder. "Come upstairs with me."

Ashley impulsively arched her head, needing Vic's lips against her flesh, seducing her into submission, trailing wet kisses and sweet suckles against her skin.

Vic's lips never touched. Hot breath spiraled against Ashley's flesh. Vic moved her mouth with aching slowness along her neck, where she finally stopped at her ear. "I want your insides quivering around my tongue again."

Ashley moaned. God, she wanted to stop the sound but it was winging against Vic's face before she could dare trap its meaning. "Vic, I...can't. We...shouldn't." Regret pierced her heart at the same time Vic sucked her lobe between her teeth.

A whisper swept against her ear. "Yes, we should. I want to be inside you."

Ashley almost swooned with the rush of fire licking her pussy.

She pulled back to look up into those eyes. The sweet pain throbbing between her legs reminded her that this gorgeous vixen could extinguish her arousal if she gave in to temptation. Vic stared at her like she was tonight's special.

Helpless, and under Vic's enchanting spell, she nodded, barely holding strong to the sanity side of insane. Did she just nod her approval to a woman she ran like hell from years ago? Would the sex-starved high diminish if she changed her mind and walked away? Could she change her mind?

Heaven help her, she didn't want to. She wanted Vic delving between her thighs, pumping out her orgasm.

Afterward, she could tell Vic how fucking sorry she was, and then beg her forgiveness for using their night for her own personal gain, then, if Vic would have her, she was going to plead for anything else she'd give Ashley. A date, a fuck when her body craved release, even something as small as a phone call when she was bored or overworked.

Whatever she could get, she was going to take.

Vic gently pulled her away from the dance floor. Ashley eagerly followed her through the undulating bodies, through the double doors, and out into the lobby.

Putting one foot in front of the other, Ashley started toward the elevator, knowing Vic would follow.

As soon as the doors swished shut, there was no backing out, nor was there an exit from the woman stalking toward her like a lioness.

Dear God, what had she just gotten herself into?

CHAPTER ELEVEN

The elevator rose with little more than a muted swish. Vic's heart stuttered to be so close to the woman whose images had consumed every part of her mind for the past two years. Not a day passed without the memory, the overwhelming want or need for the author who'd fled from her house as if the devil himself pursued her.

All for the sake of her fucking career. What a pathetic excuse for a human being this bitch was. And tonight, Vic was going to play her little game. Tonight, she was going to fuck Ashley Vaughn into a boneless husk then walk away. Just like Ashley had done to her.

And she'd almost missed her chance. Heather and her "fuck" date had practically pawed each other naked while Vic scouted the crowd. Just when she decided Ashley wasn't going to show, she'd emerged like an angel. Her proximity immediately jolted the breath from Vic's lungs. She'd been thrilled when Heather had convinced her date it was time to blow the joint, and Vic was free to mosey through the crowd, pinning herself in a darkened corner to await her chance.

As she closed in on Ashley now, wedging her against the chrome panel of the elevator, she mentally growled at her weakness. How could she still want her so badly? How could she still yearn for her touch? Why did the fucking breath still catch in her throat at Ashley's uniquely intoxicating scent?

Watching Ashley move through the crowd, the enticing strips

of her dress swirling around those gorgeous legs, made Vic wonder which victim Ashley had in mind for tonight's dessert. Had Ashley spent the whole evening sizing up the guests, looking for a mark to strategically place in the scenes of her next book? Vic's lips twitched in satisfaction. She'd saved some poor soul from a heartache, that was for sure.

The object of her infatuation cocked her brow as Vic towered over her. Those eyes watched her, warm and cozy, like a soft cashmere throw on a cool autumn night. A good thing Vic knew the vixen resting beneath that tranquil gaze well enough to be on her guard. She could easily fall victim all over again if she weren't careful.

However, Vic saw something else tonight—lust, thick and sultry.

More emotions played across that expressive face—fear, longing, and need. Her prey's eyes widened when Vic closed the last step between them.

"How would you like your fuck tonight, sexy?" Vic pressed her body against Ashley, nudged her knees apart, trying to maintain the dominating role. "Hard and fast? Or soft and slow—achingly slow?"

Ashley's lips parted and a soft moan escaped.

Vic almost lost her fight for control.

She trailed her fingers down Ashley's rib cage, over her lean hips, and opened her palm against soft thighs. She lifted Ashley's leg and crooked the firm thigh over her hip, then drove against her sweet pussy.

"Please, Vic. I need to—"

She wedged her finger against those plump lips. "Shhh. Don't talk." Vic ground against her.

God, she felt brave pressed against this siren, unlike the night she'd practically jerked her away from a table then fucked her standing up in a freaking bathroom. She'd been scared out of her mind that night. And heartbroken for way too long afterward. Not after tonight. Tonight, she would regain her heart and her life.

She bit back the growl of hatred rushing like wildfire through her veins, at the spiked adrenaline at being so goddamn close to the body that haunted her dreams.

Now, knowing the evil beauty was almost putty in her hands gave her a thrill beyond description. She was positive Ashley would have the colorful words to put her emotions onto pages. No matter. Vic had the upper hand now; she knew the wicked intentions behind Ashley's moans, behind her soft panting.

The sounds of her lust filled the elevator, reminding Vic why she was here.

Vapor was born while she made love to Ashley, her fingers buried deep inside her. She hadn't been make-believe; she was real. Vic wanted her revenge, wanted to walk away from this night with her head held high. First, though, she wanted Ashley screaming and squirming beneath her.

Ashley had escaped her once. Vic would be damned if she'd elude her clutches this time. Not before she could embed herself deep inside Ashley's mind and her body. She seared with the thrill of the hunt, especially now that she knew she was a character in the single book that had flung Ashley to the top of the charts.

One way or the other, she would walk out of the Hilton with payment for her troubles years earlier, for her sleepless nights, for her bruised heart.

She'd been made a fool of, left alone, naked, her body a huge mass of achingly sweet pain. But now she wasn't an idiot, and tonight, she'd show Ashley how her imagination could bite that tight ass. Let her feel the sting of rejection.

The elevator door opened with a swish.

Vic stepped to the side, allowing Ashley the room to make that first step toward her unknowing future.

She followed Ashley out then stepped around her and led the way four doors down. After inserting the key card into the slot, the button on the door turned green, and she was aware of Ashley's penetrating heat against her back.

With as much control as she could muster, she pushed open the door, flicked on the light, and watched Ashley look around with bright eyes.

She loosed an evil smile when Ashley strolled inside the room.

After fucking the bitch breathless, she'd walk away, pride intact. She'd do it for all the other unknowing fools in the world who'd fallen victim to Ashley's schemes.

Vic closed and locked the door. She followed Ashley into the single room, toward the bed that would soon hold their thrashing weight.

She dropped the card onto the dresser then shucked off her tuxedo jacket.

Ashley's gaze dropped to Vic's shoulders, along her chest and stomach, further down her legs, and then flashed back to her masked face.

Damn, was she sizing her up, perhaps pasting descriptions into the back of her mind as they stood there? Vic almost growled with the thought. Hadn't she already done this? Hadn't Ashley already mocked her on every page of her book?

Ashley moved backward until her knees bent from the edge of the bed. With a slight quiver of her lips, she lay back on the comforter, pulling the edge of her dress up around her upper thighs, as if anticipating how Vic would take her for their last fuck tonight.

Oh, no. It wouldn't be that simple, wouldn't be that quick and easy. Only one position would do for this cheating explorer of plotlines.

Vic smoothed the mask over her head and tossed it on the dresser, then moved toward the bed and stuck her hand out in invitation.

A confused scowl creased Ashley's brow as she pulled her own mask off and dropped it off the edge of the bed. She slipped her fingers into Vic's grasp.

Vic jerked her forward until she was standing, pressed tightly against her chest. "Don't assume anything of me, sexy. You gave away your control when you stepped in the elevator. Don't forget it."

Ashley's frown deepened. "Can we talk? Please?"

Ignoring the pleading gaze, Vic twisted her arm behind her back and pushed her forward until Ashley slammed up against the wall face first. "I'm going to start by fucking you here, standing up." She pushed Ashley's hair to the side then nipped the delicate space between her neck and shoulder. "You should remember that well."

"Vic, I—"

Vic kneed her legs apart and slowly lifted the edge of her dress while she sucked the silky skin of her shoulders. She pleaded with her mind not to forget her intentions tonight. Being against this body once again was driving her thoughts away. Dammit, she couldn't forget, couldn't be enthralled with those fucking moans and desperate gulps of air.

Ashley's scent was like an aphrodisiac, seducing Vic into a state of complete arousal. With her crotch soaked, her lips sealed against silky flesh and her fingers plundering along creamy thighs, she had to remind herself, yet again, what she was doing here.

Domination. Taking control. She had to take away Ashley's power.

Ashley groaned and arched her back. She pulled her hands out of Vic's and put them both flat against the wall.

Vic gently kissed the edge of her shoulder blade and then backed away. "Take off your clothes. I want every inch of you uncovered."

Ashley hesitantly tugged the straps down her arms until the top half bunched around her hips. With a hesitant glance over her shoulder, Ashley pushed the dress down until it crumpled around her white spiked stilettos.

Vic turned away. The visuals of her trim body might burn inside her mind for all eternity. Not that they weren't now. Just the feel of her was stressful enough.

She lost the fight for self-control and turned back. Her gaze drifted down Ashley's back, along the sexy indention of her spine, over her rounded ass. A little red heart rested just above the crack of her cheeks, attached to her thong. Knowing Ashley intended someone to find it made her breath catch.

Holy shit! This was going to be torture. Pure annihilation.

But damn, was she ever going to enjoy every second of this night. She sealed herself against Ashley's naked form.

The game was on.

❖

Ashley almost lost her battle with her pent-up scream when Vic trapped her hands above her head and slammed against her.

Her mind flung her back into the past, to Vic shoving her against the bathroom stall, her lips parted in ecstasy.

Right now, she felt more ashamed than turned on. Vic didn't want to talk about that night. Hell, she'd all but stomped out any possibility of Ashley's apology.

Ashley was trying to understand her feelings, how Vic must have felt waking up alone, or when she read that pathetic rejection e-mail, or God forbid, how her heart must have plummeted when she read *Vapor*.

What a fucking idiot she'd been. And right now, she had a chance to put the amends into motion. That is, if she could get her jumbled mind to work.

Would Vic forgive her? Didn't Ashley deserve the hurt if she didn't?

Fingers probed between her legs from behind. Her apology flew past her lips, riding on a moan.

Vic slid along the slit of her pussy, and Ashley held her breath, spread her legs wider, willing Vic to fill her. She needed to be fucked, and hard, needed Vic's tongue seeping through her cream, and jerking a scream from her throat.

She'd thought of nothing else for way too long now. *Please, God, let her forgive me so I can endure this sexual magnitude every day of my life.*

"You ready, sexy?"

"For wh—"

Vic drilled her fingers inside. Ashley threw her head back and released a raw cry. She bit her bottom lip to stall the scream daringly close to escaping.

Vic plunged again, so deep Ashley rose up on the tips of her toes to keep from toppling backward.

"You like being fucked from behind, don't you, sexy?" Vic's thrusts slowed, then rammed again. "And writing about it."

Ashley widened her eyes, unsure how to respond. She was sure Vic didn't really expect a response, and for some sick reason she was thrilled that Vic had made the comment. It meant she was pissed, and enraged. It meant maybe, just maybe, before she left this hotel room, she'd get to say how fucking sorry she was.

When Vic rammed again and spread her fingers, Ashley lost concentration. Her body tingled and burned with sweet sensations. She clawed at the wallpaper, haggard breaths ripping from her mouth while those fingers stroked her inner walls.

Vic's free hand slid around her waist, opened her freshly shaved lips, and pinched her clit.

Ashley was sure she was going to erupt into a ball of flames, positive the body could only handle so much pleasure before it combusted into a puff of smoke. Hot tears stung her lids. Jesus, the pleasure was jerking her to fucking tears, just as it had two years ago.

Her body quivered and her pussy clenched around Vic's stroking fingers. Her orgasm scrambled to the razor sharp edge.

It was too good. It was too hot. It was too fucking much to handle.

Suddenly, Ashley wanted away from the wall, wanted away from the very position that brought back way too many memories in tidal waves, where it had all begun for her and Vic.

She reached down and pulled Vic's hand from between her legs. "Vic, can we please slow down? I have something I'd like to talk to you about."

Vic kissed her shoulder and continued her harried thrusts inside Ashley's body. "There's nothing to say, Ms. Vaughn. Not a fucking thing I need to hear from you."

Fury bubbled harsh and hot in Ashley's gut. She shoved against the wall, sending Vic unexpectedly into a backward stumble. It was just the disconnection she needed. Vic's fingers fell free of her and Ashley whipped around to stare at her.

"What's your problem? Why won't you talk to me? Or at least listen to what I have to say?"

Anger and hurt sparked in Vic's eyes. "The only thing I want to hear coming from that mouth is your orgasmic screams."

Dear God, Vic was so hurt. It was shining bright in her eyes no matter what hard persona she was trying to portray. It didn't fool Ashley. If only she hadn't walked away, if only she hadn't been a spineless twit who was afraid of love...if only. Hell, Vic hadn't been offering her love. She'd been offering incredible sex. Nothing more.

Ashley reached out and caressed Vic's cheek. Vic jerked back as if stung.

"Please talk to me, Vic."

Vic slowly shook her head. Ashley swallowed the lump forming in her throat.

So much hurt and so much resentment. The realization stabbed Ashley. She'd done this with her cowardice, with her driving need to succeed...and at the cost of this gorgeous woman.

"Get on your knees, Ashley." Vic took a step forward.

"No. Vic, please."

Vic took another step and Ashley stood her ground.

"Get on...your fucking...knees!" Contempt flashed in Vic's scorned eyes.

Ashley smiled and knelt. If this was some kind of revenge, let the punishment begin. When she was eye to crotch on her knees, she looked up at Vic, awaiting her next command.

"Undress me."

With unsteady hands, Ashley undid the leather belt then slid the zipper down. With only a tug, the tuxedo pants fell around Vic's feet. Ashley hooked her fingers inside the waistband of Vic's gray briefs and slid them down as well. She fanned her hands flat against Vic's lean thighs and circled them to the back until she palmed those rock-hard ass cheeks.

God, Vic was perfect. Every part of her was brick hard, and ready...and oh so tempting. Ashley wanted to start with the arch of her feet and kiss her way to the crown of her head then reverse the path with a long, wet lick. She wanted to claim her.

A woman this perfect was sinful, downright sinful. And right now, she was standing before Ashley, with her pants around her ankles, her scent triggering Ashley's sexual desire.

Vic's fingers bit into her scalp and tugged her head backward. "Make me come, Ashley."

Ashley panted, heat awakening inside her body like an erupting volcano. "I can't."

"You will. Do it, now." Vic ground her teeth.

"Oh, I'd really love to, if you'd stop breaking my fucking neck."

As if snapped from some kind of trance, Vic released her hold.

Ashley needed no further prodding. Her pussy clenched as she buried her face in the vee of Vic's thighs. She parted Vic's slick lips with the tip of her tongue until she found her hard, beaded clit.

Vic moaned and her fingers sought refuge in Ashley's hair once again. She bucked while Ashley licked and sucked, urging Vic toward the sexual abyss.

When Vic's hips jerked forward and froze, Ashley whimpered with the pulses pressing against her lips.

"I'm coming—oh fuck!"

Ashley loosed her grip on those quivering buns and drove two fingers inside her, at the same time she rose to stand face-to-face with Vic.

She sought Vic's lips and swallowed her soft cries, thrusting deep inside her convulsing depths. Vic clutched at her, her body grinding hard, her pussy a tight fist around Ashley's fingers.

Holy hell, I think I might love her.

CHAPTER TWELVE

Vic clung to Ashley, arms draped around her petite body, her pussy drenched and still tightening around those slender fingers.

She felt utterly drained, and not just from the biting orgasm. From two years' worth of unanswered questions, from holding Ashley in her arms right now, from watching her scan the ballroom for her next victim, from wishing she'd never laid eyes on the likes of Ashley Vaughn. From all the fucking hurt she couldn't relinquish.

Whatever possessed her to come here tonight? What the hell did she hope to accomplish by fucking the plot whore? It was killing her, that's what it was doing. She wanted nothing more than to lay Ashley back against the cotton comforter and make love to her, to tell her how badly she missed her.

She's a bitch and a user. I can't feel anything for her. Fuck, why do I?

Somehow, her goddamn heart couldn't distinguish between pleasure and pain. From painful pleasure.

That alone fueled her anger, and her confusion.

Ashley's tongue forced inside her mouth again and Vic could taste and smell her own arousal. She released a guttural groan, scooped Ashley up in her arms, and practically flung her in the center of the bed.

Okay, so her plans hadn't worked out quite as planned. Well, not that there really was a plan, or a damn scheme. She'd let her hormones do the talking years ago. She'd be damned if she let it shadow her common sense now. Ashley deserved to be fucked senseless and then dumped, deserved to wonder for the next two years what had gone wrong. If Vic could publish a novel about this night, God knew, she would, just to drive that nail of hurt home once and for all. But she couldn't do that. Hell, she could barely write a coherent blog, let alone describe every tiny detail for the world to see. Oh, she wished she could. God, how she wished she could.

With her sights trained on Ashley's naked form save for that thong that would be history very soon, Vic shucked out of her stiff shirt, tugged her sports bra over her head, and then went after the evil princess.

She was going to make her scream, and she was going to make her come hard, and when she lay there half-dead from hyperventilating and lack of oxygen, Vic was going to walk the fuck out of this room. And she was never going to look back.

With her head held high, she prowled across the bed and between Ashley's legs. When Ashley reached for her, Vic grabbed her wrists and pinned them on either side of her head against the mattress.

She stared down into those eyes, praying her last prayer she'd see the answer there, that the answer resting inside the bound book was a lie, some kind of horrible mistake.

"Are you ever going to talk to me?" Ashley wrapped her legs around Vic's waist and urged her forward.

Vic shook her head. "Do you always talk this much during sex?" Vic gave herself a mental slap for thinking she could find any answers behind those deceitful eyes and released one of Ashley's wrists. She slid her hand between them, down between Ashley's legs, and then snapped the delicate string of her thong in half.

"What is it with you and sexy lingerie?"

"Why is it always in my way?" While a smile tricked across Ashley's lips, Vic splayed her slit open, stroked just at the entrance, then slowly entered her. As soon as her fingers smoothed through her cream, Vic moaned, matching the sound escaping Ashley. "Jesus, you're so wet."

The sensation of those slick walls clutching at her weakened her further. What a fucking imbecile she was to think she could come here and fuck Ashley out of revenge. She had to be the biggest idiot alive.

Ashley pumped her hips, sucking Vic even deeper, both physically and mentally. "Oh, yeah, Vic. Please fuck me."

The prodding pulled Vic back to her senses. Fuck Ashley, and fuck her hard. Leave her sated, breathless, and boneless, so she could take those things back to her computer. Let her write whatever the fuck she wanted, and then let her hold those memories for life. By that time, Vic would have moved on with her life, with Ashley Vaughn nothing more than a dirty, miserable memory.

With renewed direction, she drove into Ashley, using her legs as leverage to fuck her harder and faster.

Ashley clutched at her shoulder, tightening her legs around Vic, bucking to meet her thrusts. She dug her head into the pillow, sucked in air, then leaned forward in search of Vic's mouth.

Vic hesitantly parted her lips against Ashley's mouth. When her tongue met Ashley's, she sighed and then sealed their kiss.

Ashley pulled her other hand free and palmed Vic's neck, pulling her deeper into the connection. She brushed her fingertips along both sides of Vic's face and then wove them into her hair.

Vic jerked back. No more kissing. That mouth was going to drive her into a state of frenzy. And those moans. Fuck, did she have to sound so erotic?

Ashley stared up at her, confusion crawling across her expression.

Vic ducked out of the vise grip and rolled Ashley onto her stomach so she wouldn't be tempted by those eyes, or those lips.

She kneed Ashley's legs open and pressed against that heart-shaped ass. Mistake! Her ass was just as perfect as the rest of her.

"I thought authors were supposed to have fat asses from sitting on them all day." Vic circled her hips and licked a wet trail down the enticing indention of her spine.

"You're a fine one to talk." Ashley glared over her shoulder, her lips parted as she pressed backward against Vic. "Aren't chefs supposed to be fat and flabby from eating too much?"

Vic grinned and slammed her hips forward, jarring Ashley against the headboard. "Muscle. This chef has muscles."

Ashley put her hands flat against the mattress, leveled herself on hands and knees, and rounded that fucking ass against Vic's crotch. "Then use them and fuck me!"

Vic growled as she sought Ashley's wet entrance, then rammed inside her. Ashley's hips arched, her hands shoving against the mattress to meet Vic's thrusts. Pump after pump, she drove into Ashley until their bodies were thrashing against the mattress. Her legs quivered as the muscles bunched, pain searing through her upper thighs, yet she continued thrusting forward, Ashley panting heavily beneath her.

Ashley felt so fucking good, and they fit so perfectly together, and their timing was impeccable. Why did Ashley have to fuck that up? Why did she have to rip apart something that could have been amazing?

She could feel Ashley's orgasm climbing, teetering on the edge. Her soft cries increased, her body arching, and grinding. Just when her pussy clenched, ready to send Ashley spiraling into the pleasure, Vic stopped, her fingers still filling those slick walls.

Ashley cried out, mewing like a kitten, and huffed in protest. "Vic, please. You're killing me."

No more than you've already killed every part of me.

"Not yet...give me time." Vic slid her fingers out to the tips and then pushed forward hard.

Incredible warmth spread down Ashley's spine.

Everything was too powerful, too overwhelming, and fucking hot as hell. She knew she'd never experience anything else like it for as long as she lived. Vic possessed everything she needed, everything she wanted, everything to complete her.

She had to tell Vic those things. Tell her she was sorry and beg her forgiveness.

The teasing slowness of those fingers slid out again, stopping at the very exit, and slowly filled her again. Then she felt the probing finger pressing against the puckered hole of her ass.

"Vic...don't...oh..." Ashley's nerves flared with heated awareness, and her pussy clenched and throbbed.

Vic pressed again, massaging the resisting ring.

Ashley tensed, but her body yearned for Vic to enter her, to fuck her until she cried. Her eyelids fluttered shut as she attempted to relax her muscles.

Farther still, Vic pressed and circled until the tip of her thumb pushed past the resistance.

Ashley cried out, and jerked backward into Vic's body. She was burning alive, everywhere, inside and out, mentally and physically... the sweetest pain she'd ever felt. "Oh fuck...Vic!"

Vic flattened her other hand against Ashley's stomach, sliding upward until she cupped Ashley's breast. She pinched a nipple between her fingers, her thumb stretching Ashley's anus, filling her, sending commingled pleasure and pain spiraling through her core.

Ashley reached back over her head until she had thick handfuls of hair, with Vic's mouth sucking like a vulture against her neck. "Faster. Fuck me harder!"

Vic reversed her slow glide then kicked up a steady rhythm, thrusting roughly on the in stroke, gentle on the out stroke. She released her clamp on Ashley's nipple and moved down between her thighs. While she lightly flicked Ashley's clit, those fingers stroked inside her ass, inside her mind, gradually kicking up the speed, practically driving her out of her wits.

"You feel so fucking good." Vic circled the tip of her finger against her clit. "Scream my name, Ashley."

Ashley sobbed, her body so alive and incredibly awake with sensations she never knew existed. Her body vibrated, and burned everywhere; it was burning so fucking sweetly. Tears fell over the brink as Vic thrust inside her, reaching her very soul. She cried from the emotion, for her loss, for Vic's bruised ego, from the pleasure, for only God knew what else.

Her orgasm spiraled to the edge, seesawed, was yanked back, and shoved to the brink again, leaving Ashley in a complete state of wet need.

And finally, her orgasm scrambled forward and showered her into the abyss. She screamed Vic's name, clawing at her hair, her body on fire, and cascaded in unbearable prickles of heat. Her orgasm clamped tight, over and over, pumping through her body in exquisite waves of fire and splendid pain, and dear God, it was gut wrenching. Convulsions swept down her body followed by quivers as her insides pumped with strong contractions.

She thrashed against Vic's solid form, her insides clenching tightly around those fingers. "Ohgodohgodohgod."

After what felt like half an eternity, her body sagged. She slumped in Vic's arms and released her death grip on her hair. Vic held on tight and gently laid her onto the mattress.

She spooned in behind Ashley and brushed sweat-soaked hair from her face. She was vaguely aware of her body tingling, almost numb, of the soreness already trickling through her muscles, through her bones.

I can't love her. She hates me.

❖

Vic sat in the chair at the end of the bed watching the heartless sleeping beauty twitch in her slumber. It was cute how her brow creased, how a smile continued to drift lazily across her lips. Had she watched Vic the way Vic was watching her now? Or had she been too intent on making her escape while Vic dreamed of their night together?

She was fucking beautiful. Too bad she was ugly beneath and that Vic had seen her true colors. Too bad she'd used their night to boost herself forward. What a shame Vic happened to love her, or at least the notion of what could have been.

How could someone so angelic be the devil beneath? How could anyone, ever, be so cruel? How the fuck could she still want Ashley after seeing the real person behind the sham?

Hot tears stung her cheeks. Vic roughly swiped them away. Their wetness only broadened her irritation and annoyance. Actually, it enraged her. Ashley didn't deserve a single tear, let alone the years she had devoted to thinking about her.

Yet Vic could feel more tears gathering like a tidal wave, threatening to overtake her if she didn't get the hell out of this room, away from the glorious body lying in an edible heap against the mattress with one delicate foot sticking out from under the sheets.

Vic shook her head, unable to believe how weak Ashley had made her, and pissed. Pissed because of her weakness, and angry with herself for being weak enough to cry. She didn't cry—ever—and she definitely wasn't weak.

Ashley was making her eat those facts. Right now, she was both. A freaking weak loser of a crybaby. What a marshmallow she was becoming.

She pushed away from the chair and stood over the bed. Ashley had pulled the pillow against her stomach, holding it like she was familiar with the act.

The thought thrilled Vic for some reason. As mad as she was, the thought of someone else fucking Ashley the way she had, draining her into a deep sleep, drove her out of her mind. Actually, the thought was downright sickening and unnerving and made rage bubble like a hot sulfur spring in her gut.

She'd fought against those very thoughts for so long.

Ashley sighed in her sleep and curled deeper into the pillow. Vic wanted to strip her clothes back off and trade places with that lucky feather-filled sack.

As soon as the image sputtered through her mind, Vic quickly turned away. Hell, she was sicker than Ashley Vaughn. After everything Ashley had done, she still wanted her, still clung to the hope that something could ever be alive between them.

What a sick sap she was to even dream of such madness.

Ashley was like a demonic black widow; she'd caught Vic in her web and trapped her there for all time.

This night was supposed to solve her problems, to set her free of the hurt, of the anger, of the resentment and the unrequited love she'd carried for far too long.

Hadn't she just fucked Ashley into a semi coma? Just as planned?

Why was she still standing here pondering the what-ifs, and what could have been, when there wasn't anything to be pondering to begin with?

Vic stomped back to the chair and jerked up her tuxedo jacket. It was time to finish this, time to leave Ashley high and dry just the way she had left Vic.

Vic's fingers closed around the jacket and she turned to barrel through the door. Something prompted her to turn back for one last look at the woman who'd stolen two years of her life.

Would Ashley even give a shit? Would she give this night a second thought? Would she be as confused as Vic had been?

With her heart dragging like a lead weight, she knew Ashley wouldn't care. A woman like her didn't have a heart to care, didn't have the conscience to worry about other people's feelings. Her life revolved around me, me, me.

She turned toward the door, determined to get as far, far away from Ashley as possible.

"Where are you going?" Ashley's voice was hoarse and crackled.

Vic turned back around, deliberately slowly while she got her brain functioning. She missed her chance to play out this part of the plan. She'd stayed too long watching Ashley, toying with the same unanswered questions she'd been asking herself for two years too long.

Why did she think she'd get answers while watching her sleep?

One look at Ashley's disheveled hair and her mind went blank. And rage took root once again.

"You weren't thinking about sneaking out on me, were you?" Ashley grinned and patted the bed in invitation.

Against her better judgment, Vic let her need for answers draw her back into Ashley's clutches. "Why? Isn't that what you did to me?"

The soft expression left Ashley's face. "Yes. That's exactly what I did to you." She sat up on the bed with her back against the satin headboard. "Go if it will make you feel justified."

"Justified! How dare you talk about justification?" Vic ground her teeth and gripped the jacket in a tight fist. "There's not one fucking thing that could justify what you've done."

Ashley broke eye contact and looked away. "You're right."

"You're heartless!" Vic took one deliberate step toward the bed, not afraid she'd unleash pent-up anger. She was afraid she wouldn't.

"You're right." Ashley met her gaze once again and tears glimmered in her eyes.

"You're a fucking plot-seeking loser."

Ashley nodded. "I am that, too."

Confused, Vic started pacing. She hadn't expected Ashley to be so calm with her outburst. Not that her plans had included this particular outburst. She now wanted Ashley to argue, wanted her down on her knees, begging and pleading with her tongue, lips, and fingers.

"You're a heartless she-devil, that's what you are."

Ashley arched a brow. "I'm not heartless, Vic."

Finally, something she could lash out at, something to fight. "You're evil and I wish I'd never laid eyes on you." She took another step, entirely too close to that naked body draped in the thin sheet. "Touching you tonight made my skin crawl."

Ashley's eyes widened and she looked down. "Wow. I'm sorry to hear that. I'd never have guessed. You set mine on fire."

Vic swallowed and images raped her mind of Ashley thrown against her chest, arching, her insides pulsing and gripping around her fingers.

She wanted to do it again. God, how pathetic, but she wanted Ashley curling around her face right this very second. "Why, Ashley?"

Ashley shrugged. A tear slid down her cheek. Vic suffered the urge to go to her, to pull her into a hug, to kiss away that frown.

"That's all I get? One fucking shrug?" Vic waved her jacket in the air. "You plaster every last detail of our night in a goddamn book, and that's all you can come up with? A measly shrug? You're more deranged than I thought you were."

More tears slid down Ashley's face as she looked up. Those eyes nearly jerked Vic into those arms. "I...I couldn't let..." She rubbed her hand across her cheek, only managing to smear a dark streak of mascara under her eye. "I couldn't let that night die."

Confused, her senses on high alert, Vic sat on the edge of the bed, fearful her legs couldn't hold her upright with whatever Ashley was going to say. "So you sold it to the highest bidder? Couldn't you just jot it down in some girlie diary?" Vic leaned forward, pasting Ashley in a death glare. "And what about tonight? I watched you looking over the crowd like a hungry predator. Which victim did you have in mind before I showed up, Ashley?"

Ashley's head shot up, her eyes wide with confusion. "Victim? What the hell are you talking about?"

"Tonight's fuck. The poor sucker who would have wound up with a starring role in your next book. Just like I did."

Ashley's expression darkened. "Is that what you think I do? What you think I did?"

Vic nodded, her jaw achingly tight. "Isn't it?"

Ashley pushed away from the headboard, the sheets spilling around her legs. She crawled to Vic then cupped her cheeks.

Vic jerked back but Ashley wove herself into her lap to straddle her. She forced Vic's head back around. "Listen to me, dammit! I'm sorry. Sorry that I couldn't let that night die, that I wrote a novel out of it, that I was a coward and ran like hell." She looked down. "I can't undo anything I've done, Vic."

"No shit!" Vic attempted to push Ashley off her lap, but Ashley grabbed her wrists in a firm grip.

"Please listen to me. Forgive me, I beg you. I never meant to hurt you, never expected New York to give me a shot, let alone offer me a contract."

"So?" Vic succeeded in thrusting Ashley away and slid off

the bed. She needed room, needed all her wits to finish this, and Ashley's closeness wasn't helping. "That doesn't explain why you wrote all those private details down for the world to read and then hawked them around until you found a buyer."

"It wasn't like that."

"Then tell me what it *was* like." Vic paced back and forth barely keeping her temper in check. "I'm a bit confused here. You wrote a book based entirely around our night together then sent it off to a publisher, or publishers. And you expect me to believe some fairy story about how *you didn't mean to hurt me*?"

Ashley crawled back to the headboard and pulled the sheets around her. "Hurting you was the last thing I wanted to do."

"Really?" *You could have fooled me.* "Let me get this straight. You wrote all that stuff, accepted a contract, because you *didn't* want to hurt me?" Vic forked her fingers through her hair. "I'd really hate to see what you do to people you *do* want to sabotage."

Ashley buried her face in her hands, quiet sobs shaking her body.

Vic only watched, forcefully rooting her feet in place. She'd be damned if she comforted Ashley, or fell into whatever her game was. She was an author; surely that involved some natural acting as well.

When Ashley looked up, mascara in wet lines down her cheeks, it was all Vic could do to stand her ground. "I was terrified."

"Of what?"

Ashley twisted the sheet in her fingers. "You."

Shocked, Vic took a step back. "Me? What in the hell for?"

"Of what you made me feel."

Vic angled her head to study Ashley's face. She looked genuine, but was she? Was this some kind of game? Was this how she sucked in her victims? Hadn't she already pulled Vic down into a morass of emotional turmoil?

Vic felt no closer to the answers than she had two years ago, only hours ago. More questions formed in her mind.

"Explain. I'm running out of patience."

Ashley pulled her knees to her chest and folded her arms around them, like a protective cocoon. "I can't explain it, dammit. That's what I'm trying to tell you."

"You aren't telling me anything, just babbling about shit that makes no sense." Vic moved to the window, afraid she'd reach for Ashley, that Ashley would welcome the embrace, or worse, push it away once again.

"Fuck!" Ashley slammed her hands against the mattress. "I was afraid, okay? Afraid of my feelings for you. They were too strong, too sudden, and too unreal. Love was something that happened between the pages of a book, not in real life, and certainly not to me. Every time I get close to somebody I get hurt, so I tried to write my feelings away, to protect myself from hurt, but it didn't work. I'm still tortured by what might have been."

Vic felt like Ashley had punched her in the stomach with her admission, with her lies. Here she thought she might get some inkling of an answer, and instead, Ashley was trying to suck her right back in to her dark pits of plotting hell.

She stared in her astonishment at the lies Ashley could so easily whip up. Her imagination was far greater than Vic assumed.

Vic watched as Ashley slid off the bed. She truly thought Vic was a moron, that she was desperate enough to fall back into her trap. The bitch had some nerve.

When Ashley stopped in front of her, Vic stared down into those eyes, seeing the monster for what it really was.

"I don't know how to make things up to you. I'm begging for a chance to figure it out." Ashley cupped her cheeks. Vic resisted slapping the touch away. "Please. I'm asking you to give up a few weeks of your time to spend with me so I can attempt to right this wrong."

Hadn't she already given up two years? Hadn't she already given a big chunk of her heart?

Hell yes, she had. But somehow, more time with Ashley felt right, felt wickedly right.

Biting back a snicker, Vic nodded. A few more weeks in

Ashley's bed, fucking her senseless, drawing her into Vic's own little game? What could it hurt?

It couldn't. It wouldn't. Quite the opposite.

And when she had Ashley deep in her clutches, she'd set her free. In the very same fashion she'd set Vic free.

What a sweet conclusion Ashley was handing her.

Vic nodded.

Ashley slammed against her and wrapped Vic in her arms.

Oh yeah, dive right in, baby.

Welcome to my game.

CHAPTER THIRTEEN

Vic unlocked the back door of the restaurant that led directly into the kitchen and stood to the side while Ashley walked inside. Two weeks had flown past, with Vic charming and wooing Ashley every step of the way.

The first few days had been the hardest, when she couldn't bear the thought of touching Ashley, let alone waking up beside her. Now, it was becoming entirely too easy.

Ashley looked around, her eyes wide with amazement. "I've never been inside a five-star restaurant before my night with you, let alone in the heart of a chef's domain. It's so bright and clean in here."

Vic grinned and led the way to the stainless steel island counters dividing the room in half. She was proud of her accomplishments. As far as she was concerned, all of her dreams had come true save for one—finding that one special person to share it all with. Although she'd hardened her heart to Ashley, her words found a way inside to boost her ego.

Ashley laid her purse on the lower shelf and turned to Vic. "Are you really going to let me cook? I did warn you that I can burn water, right?"

Vic nodded and went to the double refrigerator. She removed two store-bought sausage links she stored for the late nights poring over last minute computer stuff. "Yes, you did happen to mention that over dinner last night. Makes me wonder how you've managed not to starve yourself to death. You could well take some tips from Caprice."

Vic almost cringed at how easily Ashley's best friend's name slipped from her mouth as though she were familiar with talking about the people Ashley loved the most. She had to admit she enjoyed the cookout with Caprice, her husband, and their adorable children. That was the one true time throughout her weeks in Ashley's company that had pulled her heartstrings tight. She didn't want to know that soft side of Ashley, to get involved with her life. Meeting those people whom she cared about made matters worse, as though she were somehow connecting with the deepest part of the conniving author.

Worse, she truly liked them, right down to the rowdy boys that Ashley adored. It had been priceless watching her sneak them candy bars when their mother wasn't watching. They'd taken off to their video games with mischievous smiles playing along their lips, snickering that they'd gotten away with something so naughty. Vic was sure that little game was routine, something those boys would never forget about their aunt Ashley, and positive Caprice had eyes in the back of her head. Ashley wasn't getting away with anything. Caprice was only letting her think she was. Vic didn't have to be a mother to see those facts.

And to make matters worse, Caprice's husband was about as cool as a straight man could get. He'd circled her car with wide-eyed appraisal, physically pouting about how Caprice had banned him from the chick-magnet mobiles. She'd been tempted to toss him the keys for a cruise, but the raised eyebrow of Caprice warned her that might be a deadly mistake. And to think Ashley's best friend was a top-notch bestselling author hadn't surprised Vic in the least, yet Caprice treated Ashley like her equal and Ashley fell happily into the role. Caprice's pride had shown brightly as they talked about brainstorming some new work in progress that Vic had quickly blocked out. She didn't want to know what truths lay behind the plotline, what other victim might soon be shedding tears when she picked up Ashley's book.

Did Caprice know the truth? Of course she did, which only

made Vic more embarrassed. A stranger knew detailed information about her sex life. Her sex with Ashley. God, it was downright harsh.

"Burger Barn and KFC are my wing men. No one could starve with them only two miles from home, or with Caprice cooking for an army. Besides, no one makes mashed potatoes like the colonel." She winked playfully when Vic caught her gaze with a stern glare. "Well, probably not like you could, I mean." She batted her eyelids and gave a schoolgirl smile.

Vic shook her head and tossed the bags on the counter beside her.

She went to the cupboard and grabbed a medium size onion and the smallest bag of potatoes she could find then carried them back. Ashley caught her wrist and Vic practically froze in place, the contact burning a path of heat straight to her crotch.

"Kiss me, oh sexy chef of mine." Ashley draped her arms around Vic's neck and pulled her down. "I've thought about those lips all day."

Vic wanted to resist her. She didn't have the ability to deal with this new Ashley. The Ashley she'd never gotten a chance to know years ago. This Ashley was playful and teasing, just the way Vic liked her women; it was unsettling.

As their lips touched softly, she reminded herself this was a game, one that she was playing wisely, and with perfection.

So what if she got to steal a few kisses here and there? So what if she could fuck Ashley every chance she got? So what if she'd never see Ashley's wonderful family ever again? Wasn't that part of the whole process? Wasn't it a small price to pay for bittersweet revenge?

Ashley's tongue curved across her bottom lip before she sucked it between her teeth.

Vic closed her eyes at the same time she sealed her lips against Ashley's. Their tongues met and curled around one another.

Her body automatically heated when Ashley moaned and palmed her hand flat against the nape of Vic's neck. For some awkward reason, her libido had a mind of its own in Ashley's grasp.

Her caresses felt so real. Her kisses felt anything but fake. Everything about her felt incredibly genuine as if she truly were giving this so-called relationship everything she had.

If only that were true. If only. Vic knew better, and she'd be damned if she let those feminine sounds snag her sanity.

She palmed Ashley's ass and lifted her legs around her waist before placing her on the counter. With practiced skill, she tore at her shirt and silky bra until creamy flesh filled her hand, the pebbled nipples hardening against her palm.

She thumbed the jeweled creations and wondered how a body could be so amazing, how someone could be so sexy.

Ashley drew back from her touch and reached for Vic's shirt. Vic pushed her hands away. "I want you pumping against my tongue."

Ashley whimpered. "Fuck almighty! I want myself pumping on that tongue of yours too."

Vic snagged at her jeans until the zipper lowered with a growl. Ashley lifted her hips and Vic slid the denim and thong down just past her knees.

"Is this sanitary?" Ashley tried to kick the jeans off but Vic grabbed her legs and lifted them until they rested around her shoulders, with Ashley's ankles locked in place by her jeans.

"Do you give a shit right now?" Vic buried her face in the creamy wetness and lapped at her clit.

Ashley jerked forward. "Oh, fuck…hell no!"

Vic couldn't get enough of her. Her taste, her scent. She'd have to learn how to fight harder against Ashley's natural aphrodisiac.

Then again, the more she made Ashley weak, the further into her trap she'd drag her down. Right? Yes. Fuck her. Fuck her hard. Fuck her over and over. Make her dependent. That was the name of this game.

With that final thought, Vic drew her clit between her lips and nursed, flicking her tongue against the swelling bud. Ashley cried out, holding herself up with one hand, the other buried in the strands of Vic's hair.

Vic watched her, took in every last detail of her features: her brow creasing, her lips parting, the cords of her neck muscles quivering as she tossed her head from side to side, her nipples hardening tighter against the cool kitchen air.

Just as her insides pulsed once, then twice, Vic searched her opening then pushed two fingers inside. What she didn't expect was Ashley throwing her head forward, her orgasm pulsing with strong convictions against Vic's mouth, and her gaze locked with Vic's. Her mouth parted, and she was coming. And she was watching Vic while she came.

Vic almost hurled back from such a precious moment. Dear God, she'd never had anyone stare at her while her body cascaded over the razor sharp edge. Not like that, anyway.

Finally, Ashley closed her eyes and sank onto her back against the cold metal counter. Her body convulsed as her orgasm slowly diminished.

Only when Ashley stilled did Vic remove herself from the confinement.

She hovered over her, unsure what to say, or what to do.

For some reason, she didn't feel like she'd just fucked Ashley. That felt more like making love. The way Ashley had watched, it was priceless. She prayed the memories would forever scald Ashley.

Vic almost snickered at the final thought. What other reason would Ashley have to watch that precise moment? She'd only been memorizing the details, pasting them into the back of her mind so she could bring them back to life with her keyboard.

What a moron she was to think anything less. Ashley needed the analysis for her next book. Vic had no doubt she would find this exact scene in Ashley's newest creation.

The thought was disturbing. She swallowed a hasty growl just thinking about all the plots she'd been giving Ashley over the past few weeks.

"I should stamp a trademark on that tongue of yours." Ashley pulled herself into a sitting position. Her hair fanned around her face, her nipples nothing more than hard, dark pebbles.

Vic helped her right her shirt before helping her down to her feet. "How do you know someone else hasn't beaten you to that task?"

Ashley quirked her brow. "You better watch it. I know people. Low-life people. For five bucks and a pack of cigarettes I could have that..." She delicately tapped her fingertip against Vic's bottom lip. "...tongue stuffed and shellacked...and tucked into my nightstand."

Vic roared with laughter. "I'll keep that in mind."

Ashley gave one stiff nod. "You do that."

Vic's smile was still broad when she washed her hands, then went to the oven against the side wall. She grabbed a pan from the rack hanging above, then she reached for the olive oil from the bottles lining the back of the stove. "First, we have to grease the pan."

Ashley wedged in beside her. "Hold up. Why don't I get a chef's hat?"

"Because I'm the chef."

"But you don't have a hat either. We have to have the proper props."

Vic reached around her and plucked an apron from the coat rack. "Here, will this do?"

Ashley eyed the material then shrugged. "I guess, but I think I'd look adorable in a chef's hat." She curved her bottom lip into a pout.

It was the cutest thing Vic had ever seen. She moved around Ashley and pulled a linen drawer open. She withdrew two white hats then handed one to Ashley while she donned her own.

"There. You happy now?"

Ashley's grin broke across her mouth as she fluffed out her hair then pulled the hat on, stalling to cock her hip to the side, her hand against her cheek, and those delicious lips puckered in a kiss. "How do I look?"

Adorable. Fucking sexy and adorable. Vic grabbed her waist and pulled her into a kiss. Ashley molded her body against Vic and wound those lean arms around her neck while she released a slow hum.

The sound vibrated against Vic's lips and she pulled back. She had to get control of herself. Dammit! She was getting too comfortable.

She turned to the pan and flicked on the burner. "Okay, chef, time to get cooking. Your job is to wash the potatoes. There's a bowl right beside the sink."

"Cool. Point me to the sink."

Vic eyed her and then looked at the sink only ten feet away, a smile threatening. "You do know what a sink looks like, right?"

"Don't play smartass with me." Ashley followed her gaze then walked to the triple sinks with a ceramic wall separating each bowl. "Holy cow. You call this a sink? I could do backstrokes in this sucker."

"Let's not. That really would be unsanitary." An image of Ashley bucking against her mouth shot across her mind. She gripped the edge of the stove.

Why the hell weren't things going as she'd planned? Fuck her, suck her into the game, and then leave her. Simple step-by-step procedure. Why in the hell couldn't she get just part of the plan right?

She pushed away from the oven, grabbed a cutting board from the lower shelf then slid a kitchen knife from the wooden holder on the counter. While she peeled the onion, she watched Ashley's hips sway as she dunked each potato under the cold water before she dropped them in the bowl. Sexy, and lean…she was mesmerizing.

Vic wanted to go to her, bend her over the edge, and then fuck her until her legs gave out.

Pain seared her finger. She jerked back and dropped the knife, automatically shoving the tip of her finger into her mouth.

Ashley spun around then raced around the counter. "Let me see." She withdrew Vic's hand from her lips, pulling her back around the island.

She plucked a paper towel from the holder above the sink and pushed Vic's hand under the stream of water. "I guess this means I get to be the chef, huh?"

"Not on your life. It's just a prick." Vic eyed her finger more closely to make sure.

Ashley finished rinsing the cut then wound the paper towel around it, adding pressure. "You're right. It's just a prick, you big baby." She winked and released her hold. "Point me to the Band-Aids."

Vic nodded toward the swinging doors leading into the main dining room. "First aid kit on the wall beside the door."

Ashley gathered some items then returned. "Are you always this clumsy in your own kitchen?" She made sure Vic's finger was dry, added antibiotic ointment, then wrapped a fingertip Band-Aid around the end.

"Only in the presence of sexy women."

"And how many 'sexy women' battle wounds do you have?" Ashley tossed everything in the trash and dared Vic to answer with a cocked eyebrow.

Vic went around and picked up the knife then carried it to the sink. After a quick dunk in scalding hot water, she dropped it in the sanitizer, picked up the bowl of potatoes, and retrieved a new knife.

"I have to count them all?"

Ashley angled her head and studied Vic's face. "You don't have any, do you?"

"Not a damn one until now." She grinned as she artfully sliced and diced the onion like the master chef she was.

"I am honored to be your first." Ashley pressed her lips against Vic's cheek. Vic feared she'd slice her finger clean off her body. Never had a woman driven her hands to shake, or made her knees so weak.

She cleared her throat, carried the cutting board to the heated oil, and scraped the onion into the pan. "Okay, while those cook, we can cut up the potatoes and sausage."

Vic took one of the packages and handed another to Ashley.

She carefully removed a knife from the holder. "Are you mature enough to handle one of these?" She rolled the knife over in her hand with ease until the handle was facing Ashley.

"Hmmm. I'm not so sure I'm brave enough to handle the chef's…equipment." Ashley teasingly wedged herself against Vic. "Can I just watch you? Might spark a plotline for voyeurism."

Vic could feel her wall crumbling. Ashley was going to break her down before this game was over. Maybe it was time to think about concluding things a bit earlier. If the charade continued this way she was going to find herself right back to waking up alone. And wondering what the fuck she'd done so wrong.

Vic swallowed and tore open the package.

"You're seriously feeding me store-bought meat? What happened to that masterpiece your chefs whipped up for us that night?" A clouded haze crossed her eyes and Ashley looked away.

If Vic didn't know any better, she'd swear there was regret and guilt gathering in that downcast expression.

"Not all chefs have to make artwork with every meal. It's nice to just throw something together for a change. Something cheap and easy."

Ashley looked up, her playful smile back on her face. "Are you calling me cheap and easy?"

"Are you cheap and easy?"

Ashley eyed the diced sausage, took a deliberate, deep inhale of the aromas already filling the kitchen, and then nodded. "For your cooking, absolutely."

Even with such a quick preparation, Vic found the closeness claustrophobic. She breathed a sigh of relief when she spooned their food onto the plates and removed her hat.

"Wait here. I have more things to set up." Vic picked up the plates and carried them through the swinging doors into the dining area to the table she had set for two. She set them down opposite each other then lit the tapered candles.

The room was dark except for the flames flickering, and the blinds had been drawn.

She rushed back to Ashley, plucked off the hat, covered her eyes, and then slowly led her back to the table before she lifted her hands.

A smile crept across Ashley's face before she turned and molded her lips against Vic's. "This is perfect. You're perfect." She sat before Vic could assist.

Ashley didn't have a clue just how perfect things were. She was playing into Vic's plan like a dream. Soon, very soon, she would walk away and leave Ashley Vaughn a whimpering disaster.

God, she couldn't wait to see the hurt crawl across her face. Ashley deserved as much. Vic had sheltered that same hurt for far too long.

It was time to give a little back to the wicked witch.

Vic pushed away the thoughts for now to focus on the moment. She sat across from Ashley. They fed each other, laughed, and teased until they were both too full to eat another morsel.

Ashley leaned back in her chair and tossed the cloth napkin on the table. "I'll never look at sausage and potatoes the same again. That was the best meal I've ever had the pleasure of tasting."

Vic propped her elbows on the table and rested her chin against her fist. "Thank you. Glad I could satisfy your...appetite."

"I watched you."

Vic narrowed her eyes. "Watched me?"

"From across the street." Ashley pointed to the window where the blinds shut out the view of the world beyond. "I was so upset when *Vapor* came out. I knew I'd made a mistake. I wanted to talk to you, to see you...to explain."

Vic was suddenly confused by the admission. "Why didn't you just call me?" She wanted to stomp out the question as soon as it left her lips. Christ, she didn't want the answers. Didn't want Ashley to say one single thing that might change the course of this game. Whatever she'd done, it'd been for her own achievement, not for Vic's sake.

"Because I'm a chickenshit."

Vic had heard enough. There wasn't anything Ashley could

say to change her mind, to change her heart. She was more than chickenshit, she was an evil temptress who'd played her game exceptionally. She was trying to do it now. Vic couldn't allow that.

She rose and tugged Ashley from the chair.

Leaving the dishes for the morning crew, Vic led Ashley to her office where she had a pallet of blankets already laid out. The room smelled of jasmine. Soon, the erotic aroma of sex would mask the exotic fragrance. Ashley cooed when she saw the candles lapping shadows inside the glass jars then lowered her body onto the blankets.

Vic dragged her shirt over her head and slipped out of her pants then joined Ashley. She needed the witch bucking beneath her. Needed to rip screams from that delicate throat.

Ashley reached for her. Their lips met in an electrifying surge of currents and then they were tearing at each other, Ashley's shirt tossed to one side, her jeans in a heap above her head, their underwear somewhere in the room.

Only when Ashley was naked did Vic stop to take in the beauty of her body. She was truly a magnificent creature to look at. What a shame there was such an ugly core beneath such a scrumptious form.

As Vic lowered herself on top of Ashley, she entered her with her fingers in one slow thrust.

Ashley's eyes fluttered shut and her head dug down into the blanket. She moaned and gripped Vic's shoulders tight. "You feel so good…make me feel so good."

Vic kicked up the speed until Ashley's body was jolting against the floor. Her own orgasm scrambled to the edge as Ashley loosed those sharp cries, her entire body wrapped around Vic like a monkey on a tree branch.

She whimpered and Vic swallowed hard and rammed inside her.

"I'm gonna come, Vic. Oh God, you make me come so hard." She bucked to meet Vic's thrusts.

Vic's insides clamped tight. "Look at me, Ashley." She rammed, hard, and then withdrew to the edge of her slick pussy. Her leg muscles quivered as she held herself poised over Ashley's entrance. "Watch me come."

When Ashley opened her eyes to stare up at Vic, Vic shattered. She held that gaze while her pussy spasmed, while she slammed deep into Ashley.

Ashley screamed out and her pussy gripped tight, followed by those familiar pulses of her orgasm.

Vic fell over her, pumping and trembling. Sweat covered her body in a fine sheen, yet she continued finger fucking her, sliding easily into her depths. She sucked at Ashley's salty neck, arching for leverage, fucking her like she might never get another chance.

Soon, Ashley was going to love her.

Soon, Vic was going to drop her like a hot plate from her very own oven.

CHAPTER FOURTEEN

Ashley couldn't remember being happier, or so relaxed. Vic was the reason for her tranquility. She never dreamed her life could be this way—with a smile plastered on her face at all times, yearning for Vic's touch every second they were apart, craving her company.

She hummed a cheerful Beatles tune as she closed her work files, careful to save all changes in the Excel document for the new clients she'd easily snagged last night during their Internet consultation. After transferring the proposed numbers over to her jump drive, she composed a new e-mail for her boss with the client's name and address then attached the worksheet.

Two months had whirled past in a hazy fog following their night at Vic's restaurant. Almost too fast. Absolutely too fast. Vic was so amazing. Ashley had hunted for even a miniscule imperfection, but if there was one, she sure as hell couldn't find it. Daily, Vic made her smile with her silly texts and frequent e-mails about nothing in particular at all. Nightly, she left her crying and sated, and splendidly drained from the sexual intensity. And weak from the emotions that grew stronger by the day.

Perfect. The woman was fucking perfect.

And Ashley couldn't be more ecstatic.

Everything was almost too good to be true, and that alone made the fear come to life every time she and Vic were apart. Was she getting in over her head? Would Vic suddenly decide Ashley wasn't for her? How would she take the rejection if or when it came?

After all the years of believing love was a farce, that it could only be brought to life with monitor and keyboard, here she was head over heels in lust.

Ashley shook her head as she looked over the e-mail once again before clicking the send button. She removed the jump drive and tossed it on the coffee table. What she was feeling wasn't lust. It was love. Incredible, spellbinding, love. And it was marvelous, toe-curling, and dear God, so heart melting.

Did it truly exist after all? Of course it did. It had to. She could feel it like puppet strings guiding her, always leading her straight to Vic. It felt great not to constantly fight the inevitable, so wonderful to let her fears float away.

She quickly looked over her schedule for the following day to make sure she hadn't overlooked an important meeting, then she relaxed. Now her night was free. Free to spend it wrapped in Vic's arms.

With work out of the way, she opened the media player, slid the headphones on, and then opened her newest manuscript. As all of her manuscripts did since Vic appeared in that bookstore, this hero possessed similar features as Vic. She'd become accustomed to changing their eye color, as well as the hairstyle, but they were always butch, and always the gentleman, and always tamed the untamable woman. Ashley naturally was that dominant-turned-submissive heroine.

With the newest chapter open and staring at her, Ashley let the tune drift through her mind, let her imagination take her to the characters where she would soon become one with each of them. She never understood how she could let the world around her fade out or how the characters lived so close to her at all times, but they did—always just a thought away. They dominated her, screamed to be heard as they clawed their way out through her fingertips.

She read several paragraphs to get back into the flow and then she was there—in their minds, in their hearts—and their story plummeted out with every stroke of the keys.

Hours later, she hit the brick wall. That wall didn't frighten her anywhere near as much as it used to, when she was torn over her guilt about Vic. She welcomed it as a necessary break from the action, especially when she was approaching the saggy middle when the action was at the bare minimum.

She saved the file, pushed the laptop onto the cushion beside her, and stretched. A quick glance at the clock on the screen told her she had about an hour and a half before Vic would leave the restaurant.

Tonight they were going to grab a bite at a little corner café, then play Putt-Putt, maybe a lazy stroll around the mall. It never mattered what Vic had planned, or if she didn't have plans at all. Just being with her was enough. Being inside her much better.

She resisted calling Caprice. The poor thing was probably sick of hearing all the sappy retells of her evenings with Vic. Though she never admitted it, Ashley was sure Caprice was waiting for the other shoe to drop, for Ashley to run screaming.

Ashley had no notion to run. She'd planted her feet firmly under Vic's table. No more running, and no more distrusting her feelings.

Love had bitten and the feeling was incredible.

Ashley frowned as a thought shimmied through her mind.

Should she confess her deepest feelings to Vic? Did she really have to? Couldn't Vic see it shining in her eyes every time they made love? Did she have to hear the words to know?

Was it the same as hearing the words? I love you.

Her heart skipped just thinking about saying those words and watching the expression on Vic's face. She would. Tonight. While Vic held the golf club, she'd whisper those sweet nothings to her. Or maybe while they cozied up at a dining table, while Vic's mouth was full, when she couldn't change the subject, something she did quite often when Ashley got a bit too sentimental. Or hell, maybe it'd be better to wait until they were both panting with sexual release? Then Vic couldn't get away.

Her heart sputtered. She loved Vic. How in the hell that had happened, she wasn't sure. Nor did she care. And right now, she wanted to say those words more than she wanted anything in her life. A thousand contracts, a hundred best sellers—nothing could compare to how those words would finally sound falling from her lips.

No. She couldn't wait.

She leaned forward and jerked her cell phone up then speed-dialed Vic.

Right now. While her heart was thundering and her mouth was drying rapidly. This very second while those words were so potent on her lips.

"Hey, sexy." Vic answered with her usual playful tone.

"I love you." Ashley shot out the words then drew in a calming breath, thankful she hadn't chickened out before the reason of sanity pulled her down into its clutches once again.

The silence drifting across the ether was deafening. Ashley squirmed against the cushions then shoved off the couch, suddenly feeling stupid and embarrassed.

Had she just pushed Vic away with her outburst, with her declaration of love?

"Say something," Ashley quietly said, then paced the length of the sofa.

"I...I don't know what to say."

Ashley twirled a strand of hair around her finger, her mouth and throat so dry she could hardly swallow.

Fuck almighty. Why'd she have to go overboard? Why couldn't she have waited for Vic to confess her feelings before she dove ass-first into the void?

"Couldn't you say I love you too? If you do, that is." Dear God, she sounded desperate. To her own ears, she sounded like some adolescent begging some punk to "go with" her.

Vic cradled the phone between her ear and shoulder, shocked into silence, her hands shaking too hard to hold the small device a second longer.

Love? Ashley loved her? What a crock of shit.

Could Ashley love anything above the number of books she

could fit on the bookstore bookshelf...the malicious way she could get them there?

She shook her head. *It's her game. She's sucking me in again. I can't let her play me for a fucking fool again.*

Besides, wasn't this really what she'd planned—Ashley wanting her? Ashley loving her?

She released an evil smile. Finally, what she'd been waiting for all along. Months of fucking her, making her bellow incoherent sounds while thrusting inside her, and finally, she'd gotten her declaration of love. And now she could tell her to go fuck herself, and walk away.

Vic opened her mouth to unleash those rehearsed words, but something clamped her mouth shut. Emotions whipped through her like a whirlwind. Ashley loved her. What she wouldn't have given to hear those words two years ago. What she wouldn't have given to know Ashley felt anything for her.

Fuck. This was harder than she thought it was going to be. Much harder than she ever dreamed it would end up.

In her mind, the words had escaped smooth as glass, with hurt sifting across Ashley's pretty eyes, her lip turning down in a frown.

But here she was on the phone, no way to see the hurt, and definitely no way to see those eyes spark with understanding.

Did it really matter? Wasn't the outcome all the same?

Honestly, she'd been playing the game for so long she'd forgotten what she was revenging. *Vapor.* Yes, *Vapor*, and her role in a bestseller. To the she-devil who ripped her heart out and tossed it on some New York publisher's desk so they could run it through a printing press, slap a cover on it, and ship it out for all the world to see. Everyone who read that book watched Vic make a fool of herself.

Anger sparked once again. With bittersweet revenge, she knew she had to finish this, to teach Ashley Vaughn how it truly felt to be used.

Something clamped sharp in her gut as she drew in an unsteady breath.

She closed her eyes and forced out the words. "I have to go. There's an emergency in the kitchen. I also have to cancel our plans for tonight."

She waited for any response from Ashley but only silence greeted her. "I also have something I want you to read later tonight... on my blog. I hope you'll find it interesting."

Vic gripped the cell phone tightly, her heart slamming like a jackhammer against her chest.

"Okay." Ashley's timid response sounded distant, quiet, as if she were a long way away.

Then the line went dead.

Vic hit the end button and chucked the phone on her desk.

God, why didn't that feel half as good in her heart as it had in her mind?

Her stomach gripped tight and she swore her throat was closing up, like her body was rebelling against her.

Dammit, why wasn't her heart jumping for joy right now? Hadn't it been twisted enough by the likes of Ashley? Hadn't it been ripped enough with every word in *Vapor*?

Yes, Godammit, it had.

She shoved catalogues and order forms out of her way and opened the Internet browser. Plates clattered from beyond her office door and hazy voices drifted down the hall from the main dining room.

This was her life, a life she'd worked damn hard to achieve, and Ashley had done everything she could to fuck with her mind.

A double-click in her favorites took her to her blog where she signed in then tapped an impatient tune with her fingers on the desk.

The story was right there. Right on the tip of her fingers.

All she had to do was write it. Of course, it wouldn't be anywhere near what Ashley could probably write, but that was okay. She didn't need perfection to seek the final piece of revenge.

Vic clicked her tongue and prepared a new blog entry.

She deserved this closure. She deserved this revenge.

Victim by Vic

I watch the conniving bitch from my darkened little corner of the ballroom. She's scanning the crowd, no doubt, searching out her victim for tonight...for the hero in her next manuscript.

I am sick and my gut cramps into a tight knot. I know the reason behind those skeptical eyes. She's searching for the poor sucker who will be the star in her next erotic bestseller. She will fuck them, draw them into her clutches, and then she will write every detail of their night together.

I know this as fact. I have been her victim.

When I can stand no more of her lethal gaze over the people, I approach her and watch her eyes widen in recognition. I wonder what's going through her mind. Is she afraid? Does she think I might spill her truth to anyone who could hear me bellow the words?

I am not fool enough to be so hasty. I have bigger plans for such an evil person.

I, too easily, talk her into a nightcap. No doubt, she sees the opportunity for another freebie outline. Of course she does. She's a smooth operator.

Once in the hotel room, she crawls across the bed while I remove my stiff jacket. I don't want to watch her. Regardless of the anger I shelter inside, she is beautiful. Her eyes are hypnotic. I can't fall victim again.

I slowly turn around.

The plot whore lies in waiting, her slinky dress like a white satin band around her hips, her legs spread wide like a cheap sidewalk hooker. She believes I am dumb. She wants me to be stupid. Her game is sweeter with the less innocent. She is smart and uses her prey wisely.

I am smarter than her now. The victims are always smarter once they survive. This time, she won't leave me *sated, or confused with emotions I've never felt before. This time it will be me who walks out that door and leaves her alone to delve into the confusion and the unanswered questions.*

Oh, but I have those answers, don't I? Those answers lie behind a glossy, erotic cover. If the world only knew the truth. I am real. I am not the fabricated story of an evil bitch.

I jerk her from the bed and push her face-first against the wall. I don't want to see her eyes when I take her over the edge. I can't see her lips part. If I could shut out the sounds, I would. I swear I would. But I can't. Those sounds I will have to endure.

Her breaths are heavy, and she wants me inside her, drilling to her core and making her scream. I know this because she's arching like a bow against me, driving me fucking crazy.

I will give her everything her body craves and much more. I will make her come so fucking hard, and I will make her cry from the intensity, and when I'm done, I will leave her. Just the way she left me.

I command her to undress herself and watch while she pushes the flimsy material off her shoulders, down around her hips, and finally in a bright white heap around her feet. She's naked save for that slinky thong with the cute red heart holding the material together in the vee of her delectable cheeks like a bull's-eye of invitation.

I look away because the sight of her weakens me— makes me want her.

I press along her contours so I can't see her body. Though now I can feel. This is much worse. When she arches further, I thrust against her and feel my guard cracking. Soon, I'm going to fall apart. Touching her drives me to my knees. I wish she knew that I probably loved her from the second I saw her across a half-filled bookstore. Probably crashed headfirst in love the second she parted those lips to release her erotic story. I was a sucker then. I won't be a sucker now.

I can't succumb to her wicked charms. I have to stay strong.

I push those dark curls away from that delicate neck and clamp my teeth against her flesh. I resist biting, hard. I would love to hear a yelp leave those lips.

I'm not heartless. No matter the hurt she has caused me, I am a gentleman. I will play this game fair. Unlike her.

Her scent is something I hadn't expected. It's an aphrodisiac. The odor is putting me in a trance. I fight off the spell while I grind against her, while I force my hand between our bodies in search of her wetness.

My knees weaken when my fingertips slip through her cream. She's wet. So fucking wet. Her own game makes her horny. How sick!

I shove two fingers inside her, so hard she lifts up on the tips of her toes. She's crying out my name. Fuck. I don't want her to say my name. I don't want to hear the sound of my name falling from those lips in ecstasy.

But there it is. And I force my thoughts away from the echo and close my eyes tight. I fuck her, thrusting in and out, over and over. I reach around with my free hand until I find her clit and I flick until she's clawing the wall with her fingernails.

For some reason, she stops me and slowly turns around. She's trying to talk. I can't hear anything else except my name still ringing in my head. I don't want to hear anything she has to say anyway. It's all lies and I know it. There is nothing she can say to take away years' worth of hurt.

I force her down on her knees and make her undress me. I want her tongue curling around me. I want her to make me come. I want her to make this pain go away. But she can't, and I know she can't. Coming is my only option, and I deserve as much.

And then I do. I come around her lips, around her tongue, around those fingers she's suddenly thrusting inside me. Fiercely hard, I pump through my orgasm.

Finally, I can think again. The rush of the moment has passed me.

And then she's standing and she's kissing me.

She tastes so good and I taste good on her lips.

Fuck! I hate her. I hate her for making me want her again, for making me forget what I'm doing here tonight in the first place.

Bittersweet revenge. I can't forget that.

I push her away and shove her back on the bed.

I need her screaming, and crying, and pleading for an end.

I desperately need those things from her. She's already taken them from me years ago.

She clutches at me, and watches me...wants me.

Those fucking eyes. Once again, staring at me, sucking me down into her grasp. Her eyes are tunnels to her lies and deceptions.

I flip her over. I can't watch anymore...or endure her kisses that I know mean nothing to her.

And then I fuck her.

I fuck her with every ounce of energy I have in my body. In every entrance, I drive myself inside her. God, she's incredible.

And she loves it, screaming for more, harder, faster. Dear God, I fucking love her.

I hang my head in shame as her pussy tightens around me, and then she's coming, her body flung against mine, arching, and grinding. Her insides squeeze me, pulling me in deeper.

She feels so good. Just like she did two years ago

when I jerked her into a bathroom stall, unable to go another second without her in my arms. We fit together then; we fit together now.

Too bad she used me. Too bad the world will never know I truly exist, that her time with me was real. Too bad she will never know how deeply I was and am hurt by her actions.

No matter anymore. My revenge is close.

And when she is drained, she all but hands a sweeter conclusion to my game on a silver platter. She has offered me time with her, faking my chance at a relationship with her. I despise how she thinks I am a moron. She thinks I will fall all over myself to get to her. She is wrong.

I take that time with great pleasure, with malicious intentions webbing through my mind.

I will lure her in and make her yearn for my touch. I will make her love me.

And I do—daily, nightly. I keep her coming back for more. I make her crave me, the way I craved her. I make her think of me, the way I thought of her. I make her cry from sexual heat, the way I cried when I cracked open my life inside the pages of her book.

And then she says the words I desperately wanted to hear so long ago: I love you.

An evil smile spreads across my lips. I have done it. I have lured the wicked monster into my lair. Now it is time to set her free, to leave her spellbound and hurting.

I fucking love her. I fucking hate her.

I fucking hate myself for loving her.

I was her victim, and now, she is mine.

The End

I only regret that I have no way to paste my story in a nice bound book for the world to see. That no one can walk into a bookstore and pluck my story from a shelf. Only an author has access to such liberties.

My mystery author will read this soon, and then she will know.
I would like to take this time to thank you for all the fucks
over the last months. It was fun pulling YOU down into MY little
charade.
Two can play your game.
Fuck you!

Vic stared at the screen, at her heartless, cruel words.

It felt good to read over them, yet her finger hovered over the mouse like a transmitter in outer space.

Her stomach physically hurt, and her heart thundered. It wasn't supposed to be like this. It was supposed to be easy, and thrilling to get the final word.

Right now, she felt like shit. Right now, she wanted to pick up the phone and call Ashley back to tell her she loved her too, that she had all along.

But Ashley's confession wasn't real.

It couldn't be.

She'd only run out of people to fuck. Out of plots to outline.

Vic couldn't be her victim any longer.

She hit the Publish button and watched while the page transformed, while her story filled in the box. While her closure whipped into a public forum.

It might not be Borders or Barnes & Noble, but it was good enough.

Even better that before midnight, the wicked plot cheater would know Vic had achieved her revenge. That Ashley hadn't gotten away with her wicked game.

Fuck Ashley Vaughn.

CHAPTER FIFTEEN

Ashley cradled the phone against her shoulder and slid a frozen pizza in the oven while Caprice read the blurb from her newest vampire story.

"His bite was lethal…and all hers," Caprice concluded.

"Bravo, bravo!" Ashley squealed though her gut cramped tight and her heart sagged as if it were already broken. Why hadn't Vic acknowledged her words? "When do I get my copy?"

"Well, considering the editor just finished the first round of edits, um, like a year," Caprice teased her. "I need a brainstorm session soon. That is if you can pull yourself away from that sex maniac of yours. I'm having a hard time feeling out my new outline for the sequel."

"How about Sunday? Vic has to work the church rush for about an hour or two. Surely we can work through your problem in that time." Ashley set the timer and poured a glass of iced tea from the fridge. Would she see Vic on Sunday? Would she ever see Vic again? From the hushed silence over the phone, Ashley had a sinking feeling Vic had just stepped out of her life without telling her.

"That's perfect. Dan wants to take the boys golfing after church."

"Since when has that sexy-ass man gotten into golf? He's so not a golfer. I see him as more of a, oh, a Hanes underwear model?" Ashley dropped onto the barstool and took a long swig. Vic looked totally edible in a golf shirt.

Caprice scoffed but Ashley knew she was smiling. She liked it that women found her hubby irresistible. "Phfft. In your dreams."

"And your point?" Ashley smiled and ran her finger down a drip of sweat on her glass, wondering if Vic had posted her blog yet. She wasn't ready to read it. She might never be ready to read it.

But what if it was the answer she'd wanted to hear over the phone? Maybe her "I love you too" would be in her blog as a poem.

Ashley didn't believe that to be true but needed to hang on to some shard of optimism or she'd be a blubbering idiot right now just anticipating what those words would say.

"Furthermore, hell, I don't know why he's got a sudden itch for such a boring sport, nor do I care. His golf gives me hours of freedom. That's all that matters." Caprice moved the phone from her ear to yell at one of the kids. "The dog's had enough snacks, he's going to explode. And for the last time, pick up those toys before I give them away to the homeless shelter. Go play something gory, or steal a car, or whatever it is you boys have on that stupid game. And do it quietly."

Ashley shook her head. "Every mother should be so proud to make their children Wii zombies."

"I've prayed. Nothing's happened yet." Caprice laughed. "Speaking of electronic devices, have you checked Vic's blog yet? Read it out loud. Every word."

Ashley rolled her eyes and slid off the stool, wondering the exact same thing for the thousandth time. She went into the living room, dropped on the couch, and then pulled the computer onto her lap. She'd been avoiding reading whatever Vic had written for the simple fact that her gut told her she wasn't going to like it. Vic had clammed up after her confession. After those sacred words she'd so stupidly admitted. Whatever possessed her to say such shit?

She only prayed Vic would forget she'd ever said them, that they could continue as if nothing was ever said.

The browser opened and she clicked Vic's blog from her favorites. A new window opened. Vic's blog was there. Dear God, whatever it was, it was there.

"It's here." Ashley's gut churned.

"Read it! Out loud."

"Victim by Vic."

"Oooh. Catchy title. Read!"

"I watch the conniving bitch from my darkened little corner of the…ballroom." Ashley swallowed, already not liking how this blog was beginning. "She's scanning the crowd, no doubt, searching out her victim for tonight…for the…oh shit."

"What? Keep reading. I already like her voice. Aside from that first-person shit I can't stand, she's got it going on."

"For the hero in her next manuscript," Ashley added.

Caprice went silent, only adding turmoil to the growing knot forming in Ashley's stomach.

"Hmmm. Coincidence. Keep going."

Ashley drew in an unsteady breath. She could feel the tears gathering against the dam. "I am sick and my gut cramps into a tight knot. I know the reason behind those skeptical eyes. She's searching for the poor sucker who will be the star in her next erotic bestseller. She will fuck them, draw them into her clutches…and then she will write every detail of their night together." Ashley clenched her eyes shut to halt the overflow. She unscrewed them and caught the next sentence. "I know this as fact. I have been her victim."

"Jesus." Caprice's single word was enough to send the first of Ashley's tears over the brink.

Without reading out loud, she let her gaze sweep steadily across the sentences, without further prodding from Caprice, until she came to the end.

She slapped her hand over her mouth to stifle a scream. The monitor blurred out of focus as more tears filled her eyes. Her heart ached so bad it was painful.

"Is it bad?" Caprice quietly asked. "Speak, dammit."

Ashley had never felt so much hatred in her life. Each word, sentence, and paragraph stabbed with deadly force.

"Ashley!" Caprice yelled.

Ashley released a sob and hugged her stomach. She rocked and let the tears flow. Her body physically hurt with the impact of

Vic's spiteful story. Their story. How could she do this? How could she write something so wicked after the time they'd spent together? Hadn't Ashley done everything humanly possible to make up for what she'd done?

"That's it! I'm coming over!" Caprice bellowed.

The line went dead.

Ashley let the phone drop from her hand and fell onto her side. She curled into a tight ball and sobbed louder. If one of those demolition balls had swung into her stomach, it couldn't hurt much less. Had anything ever hurt so bad or cut so deep?

Fuck almighty, the pain was ripping her from the inside out.

She sat up when a pang stabbed her stomach once again, her face wet, and her eyes already swelling, and pulled the laptop back onto her lap.

The heartless bitch had really fucked her. Everything she'd said and done over the past months had been for nothing. Vic's vengeful game had sucked her right into a trap until she couldn't see the path of destruction she was treading.

Vic had played her game well. Almost to perfection. Fuck, who was she kidding? She'd been perfect through every twist and turn of their so-called relationship.

Ashley suddenly felt dirty. Her skin tingled.

Vic had touched every inch of her body. She'd made her come so hard and so sweetly. She'd played her body like a musical instrument, drawing sounds and reactions like nobody before her.

And now it was gone, with nothing more than memories to carry her from this day forward.

The monitor blinked and then the screensaver flicked on.

The cover of *Vapor* floated mercilessly across the screen followed shortly by *Phantom*. She hadn't added the third cover yet, *Forever Kiss*. It would be months before she even got the first round of edits back.

Had Vic hurt like this? Had the publication of *Vapor* jerked her into this world of pain and confusion like her blog had for Ashley?

The front door flew open then slammed before Caprice barreled into the living room.

Ashley's lips puckered as soon as she saw those concerned eyes and then the tears started flowing again.

Caprice dropped her purse on the coffee table, pushed the laptop out of the way, and then plopped on the couch.

She pulled Ashley against her side and hugged her. "It's okay, baby. Whatever she said, it'll be okay."

Ashley sniffled and shook her head. "She hates me. It was all a game."

"No, she doesn't." Caprice smoothed her hair down. "Whatever she said, it was two years' worth of pent-up hurt talking. I'm still going to stomp her fine ass into a piss pool then stuff the remains into one of her Dutch ovens."

More tears flowed while Ashley ached. Ached deeper than any time in her life.

When her sobs subsided, Caprice pulled the laptop to her side. "Do you mind if I read it?"

Ashley nodded and Caprice began reading.

Ashley could hardly bear to watch, yet she couldn't bear not to follow Caprice as her eyes scanned across the screen. Every time her eyebrows arched, or a death glare moved across her face, fresh tears cascaded down Ashley's cheeks.

"Ouch! That was rough, baby doll." Caprice rubbed her leg.

Ashley buried her face in her hands. "I can't believe she did this."

Caprice plucked a tissue from her purse and pushed it into Ashley's hands. "Honey, you know I love you, right?"

Ashley sniffed then swiped the tissue across her eyes and cheeks. "Of course I do."

"Maybe she needed the closure on her own terms. I mean, you expected this from her. You said so yourself."

Ashley stared at her.

Caprice held her hands up defensively. "Don't give me those devil eyes; just hear me out. You hurt her. *Vapor* hurt her. Though you know you didn't write that book for spite, she only sees you boosting your own career. That's obvious through every sentence here." She pointed to the screen.

"I tried to make up for that! I told her how fucking sorry I was, how I wanted a chance to right my wrong."

Caprice nodded toward the computer. "Isn't that what she just did? Don't get me wrong. It was mean, and spiteful, and downright nasty, but it was her closure. She needed that to heal her hurt."

Ashley stared at Caprice and then at the laptop.

Damn, she hated hearing the truth. Actually, she wasn't debating the facts. She knew from the second the publisher offered her a contract that Vic should have been included, somehow, some way. Hell, even a phone call to let her know she'd written about true facts might have diminished the blow.

Bullshit! Ashley knew she should have dedicated the whole book in her honor. Hadn't their wonderful night together sparked the entire plotline? Instead, she'd written something smug about herself. How this was only the beginning. Never once did she think about Vic when she was signing that contract, and never once did Vic come to mind when she was staring at that hot cover.

What a piece of shit she was.

Yet she'd tried to make it up to Vic, belatedly. Hadn't she?

Hadn't the last months counted for anything? She'd spent her nights showing Vic how sorry she was, how much she cared about her. Didn't those sweet moments matter? Hadn't they let Vic see through the exterior and into her true heart?

With the laptop staring back at her, with Caprice still giving her that all-knowing frown, she knew she hadn't, obviously.

She'd wanted Vic back in her life for her own selfish reasons—for her company, for her nightly fucks.

Ashley almost swooned just thinking about the way Vic brought her body to crescendo with every touch, with every flick of her tongue. Never in her wildest dreams could she imagine her insides igniting from just looking into someone's eyes.

Vic gave her those rushed feelings. It was Vic she wanted. It was Vic she loved.

Realization slammed hard. Ashley shoved off the couch and jerked up her cell phone.

"What are you doing? Don't you dare call her!" Caprice reached for the phone.

Ashley ducked away and held up her hand then dialed her editor. She'd never dared call the overworked woman but this was an emergency. Only Janie could help her right now, and right now, Ashley needed a fucking break. She needed just one tiny thing to go right.

"This is Janie." The sweet country drawl of her editor filled the line.

"Janie! This is Ashley Vaughn. I need to ask you a very important question."

"Well, hello there, sweetie. Ask away."

"Is it too late to change the dedication in *Phantom*?"

Ashley heard the faint sound of papers rustling and then tapping of a keyboard. "Ashley, it looks like it's already gone to print."

"Fuck!" Ashley paced, scuffing her hands over her cheeks.

"I'm sorry. Is something wrong? I can call the print department if you'd like. There's a chance it hasn't hit the print press yet."

"Oh my God. Would you? I'm begging you!" Ashley folded her hand in prayer against the phone.

"I'll give it a try, but no promises."

"I'd love you forever."

Janie chuckled. "I'm your editor. You don't have a choice but to adore me. I'll ring you back as soon as I have an answer."

"Thank you, thank you, thank you." Ashley hung up and turned to Caprice.

"You can't be serious." Caprice stabbed her finger toward the laptop. "She just ditched you in a public forum and spilled your entire sex life for every blogger in the world to read."

"And? I just pasted *her* entire sex life in my book for everybody in the lesbian world to read. I didn't even fucking give her the honor of a mention on the front page."

Caprice smiled. "That was some damn hot-ass sex, by the way."

Ashley blushed. "Yes…yes it was."

"You love her, don't you?"

Ashley stared down at the phone still cradled in her hand and nodded. "I do."

"She loves you, too. I saw it. People can't hide the truth from their eyes, sweetheart."

Ashley let her mind fill with Vic's face. With those eyes. Caprice was right. Her eyes couldn't lie, no matter what spiteful game she was playing. And no matter what revenge she had on her agenda. She loved Ashley. That part of her stupid vindictive game she couldn't hide. Ashley was more determined than ever to set things right, even if doing so didn't win back the prize.

"I know. That's why I have to fix this."

"And you think a little dedication will do it? When the past months haven't?"

"Dammit, it had better." She flipped the phone over from one hand to the other, willing it to ring. "It had better."

"I'm still going to kick her ass from here to my next book signing…in freaking Florida, with all those hungry gators."

An hour later, after Caprice had left to go tend to her impatient children who were driving their daddy insane, Ashley sat cross-legged in front of the coffee table. Vic's blog stared back at her. She'd read it over and over and now could read between the lines.

Love laced around every word.

They were meant to be together. And Ashley was going to make her see that. Somehow, someway, she was going to right this wrong once and for all.

Her cell phone whistled out a tune and Ashley practically dove on it.

"Hello?"

"You're in luck."

Tears bit Ashley's lids with Janie's news. "Thank you so much."

"You have a few hours to shoot me an e-mail with your corrected dedication."

"I owe you big time."

"You can repay me with those new chapters you've been working on."

Ashley smiled. *Sweet Seduction* was almost complete. Vic had even helped her with the title, had curled right up beside her on the couch while Ashley dove into la-la land, while the character's story flowed through her fingertips.

It'd been amazing to have Vic snug against her body while the fabricated version of her cascaded into the chapters.

Vic had seemed just as content, as if she hadn't minded that Ashley was almost comatose with tunes drifting from her headphones. If they'd stayed together, that would be their life— Vic cooking delicious dinners while Ashley became one with her characters. And when the sex scenes made her crotch clench, it was to Vic's arms she could have crawled. She'd been so close.

"You got it. Two weeks, tops, it'll be on your desk."

"Awesome. Take care, sweetie."

Ashley closed the cell phone with her heart singing once again. Finally, she could give Vic what she properly deserved.

She opened a new Word document and thought about what she'd like to say. The words had to be perfect.

Vic deserved as much.

When she couldn't form the passage, she pulled on the headphones and cranked up the music. She closed her eyes and let Vic fill the void.

They were naked, and sweating. Their bodies tangled as one. Always as one.

From behind, Vic entered her and Ashley's insides coiled, tightening and convulsing around those pleasing fingers.

Ashley's clit pulsed hard between her legs with the memory.

She opened her eyes and let her fingers say exactly what she knew Vic needed to hear.

She read back over the words, then again, and once again. Were they enough?

Did they have the impact she was looking for? What Vic deserved?

At this point, she wasn't sure.

Honestly, were there any words perfect enough to open Vic back up? Had she closed their book indefinitely?

Maybe there wasn't a single dedication that would make Vic care again.

Ashley's gut churned with the thought.

She'd given up two years of life, miserable and guilty. Hell, she'd spent more time than that casting away any hope of love for fear she might find out it truly existed. And now she'd hurt an innocent person in the process. Someone she loved.

With her head held high, Ashley pulled up the blog from the bottom of the screen.

"You can write all the hateful blogs you want, Ms. Vic. You love me. And I'm going to prove it."

Ashley smiled, opened her latest chapter, and let her fingers tear through her newest work in progress.

CHAPTER SIXTEEN

Vic slammed the paint roller in the tray of rustic orange paint and stepped down from the stepladder in her bedroom. She inspected her fucked-up mess of brush marks and smudge spots where she'd accidentally bumped the wall, as well as a whole section not even touched by the roller.

Sheesh. First her cooking went to shit and now she couldn't even do something as simple as painting a damn wall.

She shook her head and slammed the ladder shut. Right now, she couldn't give a shit if the new color was triple-toned or hued with some horrendous shade of lavender. Nor did she give a piss if her jeans scraped the whole bedroom or she had brush fibers embedded in the semi-gloss.

Actually, she couldn't much care about anything anymore.

Guilt was her only companion, and she'd given a firm handshake with loneliness. Even Heather, after many months of not calling her, couldn't talk her into a quickie fuck when she stopped by the day before. God knew that miniskirt used to have Vic on her knees, seeking refuge between those lean thighs, before Heather could say please. Not this time. This time the thought only repulsed her and made her think of Ashley—how she softly cried when her orgasm scrambled dangerously close to the edge.

Vic knew with Heather's scorned expression that she'd never see her again. This time, for good. Not in the same way they'd been seeing each other for the last few years, anyway. The friendship they'd built couldn't withstand the lack of sex between them. She was sure now the sex was their only glue. It was sad that she'd be losing out on a fun and familiar friend, but she knew it was time to let loose her desperate hold on a comfy fuck.

Vic shrugged off the thoughts and yanked up the roller, tray, and coverlets spread around the floor. She left the ladder. Maybe she could use it later to tie a noose around the ceiling fan and end the torture once and for all. Not really, but something had to give on the constant throbbing in her heart.

Maybe it was best to wallow in self-pity for now. God knew it had gained a strong hold of her emotions and she couldn't feel it letting up anytime soon.

She deserved every precious memory raping her mind almost by the second, definitely by the minute. She deserved her gut clamping so tight it left her breathless. She deserved whatever turmoil her body went through. She'd played a spiteful, cruel game, and won.

Yet, winning had only made her the loser.

She trudged down the stairs and an image of Ashley, laid out delicately across the steps, wrapped around her face and pumping, came out of nowhere. Fuck if she wasn't used to those sudden memories leaping into her thoughts over the past few months.

Long, agonizing, months.

She bounded to the first floor and made her way to the garage where she stuffed the sheets back into the cubbyhole, then tossed the roller and tray into the trashcan.

What was Ashley doing now?

Was she excited that *Phantom* was about to hit the bookshelves, if it hadn't already? She'd lost track of time. Lost track of her life. Would Ashley be setting up another signing at the bookstore in town? Would she read from the pages, every other word a whisk of something purely erotic? Had she written those words the same way she had with *Vapor*?

The thought was too painful. She shoved it away before it had time to root.

And of course, Ashley would be setting up some kind of reading soon. That was an author's job—to show her face, mix and mingle with her fans, show her appreciation for the support. Vic toyed with a vision of what she'd do if she ever dared show up at one of her gigs. How she'd stroll into the bookstore and stand in the exact spot she'd occupied the first time they met, to watch and listen as Ashley wooed her and the crowd with sweet words.

She was kidding herself. She probably wouldn't step back into a bookstore, let alone anywhere near Ashley's signings or, God forbid, readings. Doing so would be too painful. It was just a pipe dream.

Vic flicked off the light and slammed the garage door shut.

Now what? Her gaze wandered around the living room. Everything was spotless, and in place. And almost everywhere she looked, something reminded her of Ashley. They'd curled on that couch. They'd fucked on that very floor. They'd kissed by the kitchen sink, and the counter, and fucked again on the dining table. God forbid she'd had to lock out every image of Ashley on those stairs.

Fuck! Her entire house was nothing more than a shrine of memories.

She could watch a movie. Or have an early lunch. Or just go back to bed and possibly inhale enough paint fumes to put her in a coma...for life.

God knew nothing else had eased this pain eating her alive by the day.

What a fucking wicked, selfish moron she'd been. She had to be the biggest idiot that ever walked the face of this earth. She mentally bashed her own head while she sank onto the couch.

Ashley had said the words she'd been so desperate to hear so long ago. Finally, her biggest wish had come true. And Vic had fucked her. In more ways than one.

Hadn't she wanted those words like nothing else in her life? Even above her own success?

She had. Yet she'd let revenge take control, to control her. And somewhere along the way, somewhere in the middle of plotting and brainstorming her wicked revenge, she'd clamped hold of love with a vengeance.

Now it was too late. She'd gotten exactly what she wished for—for Ashley to feel the bitter hands of pain.

Vic glanced at the phone cradled beside the couch. What if she called her? Would Ashley hang up after calling her every name but honey pie?

With a roll of her eyes, Vic snorted. Why the hell wouldn't she?

She slammed her head back to stare at the ceiling. Hadn't she already dialed that number a trillion times only to hang up with impatience before she could press the last button, too afraid to hear the tongue-lashing Ashley would give her? Or worse, the tongue-lashing Ashley would withhold. The very one Vic deserved.

"Fuck!" Vic rolled her head toward the bay window. The sun was bright beyond the blinds. Even the brightness couldn't cheer her up or drag her out of this self-imposed funk.

A bird landed on the feeder just beyond her porch and Vic laughed.

What kind of revenge backfired like this? Wasn't revenge supposed to feel incredibly sweet? A catharsis that freed her heart of bitterness and pain?

Obviously not her revenge, that was for sure. Her revenge seemed to have some hilarious way of calling her bluff.

Feeling horrible and guilt-ridden, Vic slowly pushed off the couch. Maybe a walk around the yard would lift her spirits. Unlikely, but anything was better than sitting here wallowing in self-pity.

She opened the front door and a beam of bright light hit her like a sledgehammer. Damn, when was the last time she'd been outside the house? Days? Weeks?

With the restaurant in capable hands, she was useless to them. Hell, she was only in their way lately. Emanuel had all but kicked her out of her own kitchen the last time she attempted to help him. She didn't want another episode like the salmon disaster, so she'd slunk back to her office to sulk where she basically stayed for the next days to come, finally opting to work from home.

A UPS delivery truck pulled to the curb so she stepped onto the patio to greet the driver, Harold. He was a pleasant older man with striking gray hair who loved showing off photos of his grandchildren.

His smile widened when he spotted her perched against the glass door. "Well, hello there, Ms. Hadley."

"Are you ever going to call me Vic?" She gave him a smile and accepted the bundle of packages. It was all she could do not to haul ass back inside. All she wanted to do anymore was curl up in bed to think about Ashley. To make love to Ashley in her daydreams.

"Sorry. Not many people indulge in first names with their delivery driver."

Vic forced a smile on her face. "That's too bad. They're missing out seeing your cute grandkids."

"That they are. And thank you for saying so." He tipped his hat. "You have a great day, Vic."

"You too." Vic ducked back into the house then tossed the packages and overstuffed envelopes onto the stand to join the rest of the mound of other mail not pressing enough to open lately.

The edge of one of the smaller envelopes caught her attention when she turned to walk away. She quickly spun back around and tugged it out from the pile.

Her knees buckled as she saw Ashley's return address label pasted in the top left corner. She turned and fell onto the La-Z-Boy as she tore into the package.

She ripped at the sides until a book fell onto the floor.
Phantom.

It was Ashley's new release.

Vic plucked it from the carpet and studied the cover. The same cover she'd seen advertised in the bookstore many months ago, the night she tried to fuck Ashley from her mind in Heather's arms.

It hadn't worked then. She knew it would never work again—with any woman.

Tears formed but she wouldn't dare let a single one loose. She refused to cry. She'd done this damage to herself, and she deserved every ounce of this ache.

As much as she wanted to open the cover, she couldn't. Not yet.

She stood and paced, turning the book over and over in her hands. Staring at Ashley's picture on the back…so fucking beautiful. Her heart constricted.

With butterflies choking the life from her lungs, she read the back cover blurb.

> *Tasha has an easy, fun life. She lives her dream of being a photographer, the only dream she's ever had. The only thing missing from the equation is love…something a bitch named Sellers ripped from her.*
>
> *Shunned publicly by the father she never knew, Sellers lives a life of partying and notching the women on her bedpost.*
>
> *The women find themselves together on a road trip from hell; hatred has never been more potent.*
>
> *Is paradise just around the corner? Or will Tasha find herself on a one-way street to the devil's lair?*

Vic breathed a sigh of relief. The hero didn't own a restaurant, or have any desire to, and the heroine wasn't a sexy lesbian erotic romance writer.

She smiled, pride for Ashley swelling her heart. Her dreams were finally falling into place.

Vic wished she hadn't screwed up her chances. That is, if those chances were real.

There was still no way for her to know, though that constant ache in her chest should be proof enough. Dammit, those words were real, they were genuine, and Vic was an imbecile.

Hesitantly, she opened the cover. The first page bore the title in huge block letters. She flipped another page and scanned through reviews for the other books distributed through the publisher. Another page only showed the title once again along with Ashley's name.

Once again, she turned the page, praying there wouldn't be a smug comment about how this book was only a stepping-stone to the next, or some bullshit like that.

She didn't know what she wanted, maybe a tiny little line in the dedication. Vic huffed in frustration. Yeah, like Ashley would waste her time to add her worthless name to her hard work.

On this page was a list of acknowledgments. She read through them, grinning as Ashley thanked her editor, and her readers, and finally, the artist who made the cover.

Her throat constricted when she flipped the last page...the dedication.

Her gaze snagged her own name like it was wrapped in bright neon lights.

To Vic: The beginning was you. You are my inspiration.
Vapor *would have never breathed life if not for you. Every book I write, you are within the pages. You are always my hero, in and out of the binding.*
　I'm so sorry! Please forgive me.
　I love you.

Vic's eyes widened in shock.

She read it again just to make sure she wasn't dreaming, or that it was her own name she was seeing.

Once, twice, even on the sixth time of reading, the dedication hadn't changed. It wasn't a figment of her imagination, and she definitely wasn't hallucinating.

Ashley had dedicated the entire book in her honor, with recognition for her role in *Vapor*.

Could she ask for more than that?

God, that was enough, and so much more.

She struggled to get her legs working and raced to her office.

A quick double-click on the icon on her desktop had her staring at Ashley's Web site in seconds.

She read through the agenda on her calendar and a smile lifted her lips.

"God, please give me a redo!"

CHAPTER SEVENTEEN

Ashley wove her way through the groups of women, stopping for small talk, answering questions, shaking hands, her ego boosting with so much praise. She was amazed to see the increase in size for her second book signing. The feeling was incredible that these people had come to listen to her reading, that they were there to meet her, that they loved her work.

She never dreamed this emotion could be so strong and now knew why Caprice was always riding on cloud nine after attending the events.

Fuck almighty, she was a published author with not one, but two books on the shelves. Giddiness raked down her consciousness as that realization found her again. Would she ever tire of this feeling? Would she ever stop slipping into bookstores just to stare at her covers?

With pride, she knew she wouldn't. This emotion was too exhilarating to fade anytime soon and she prayed she could continue writing believable plotlines to keep the readers coming back for more. She depended on their word-of-mouth promotion to increase her fan base.

Linda, the bookstore owner, moved in front of the card table. "Excuse me, ladies. Can I have everyone find a seat now?" She stalled while the crowd quieted and shuffled to the rows of chairs. "Thank you, thank you. It's so great to see such a large turnout. Ashley has promised to read us a scene from her newest release, *Phantom*. We'll have questions and answers following, as well as the signing. If anyone has brought their own books, they should have had them stamped with one of our logos when they entered. If not, please see me now so I can get that taken care of for you." She gave a wide smile and tugged her blouse over her handlebar hips. "Not that I don't trust you, but a dime is a dime, right?"

The women laughed and when no one moved from their seats, she concluded. "Then I shall get my fat butt out of the way and hand the floor over to Ms. Vaughn."

Ashley smiled as she walked away and when she looked back to the women now staring directly at her, she automatically stripped each and every one of them. She held up a copy of *Phantom* while the hair disappeared from their scalps, leaving them bald. Followed close behind were the clown noses.

The choking grip of fear subsided as she looked back over her mental creation with an impish snicker.

"Thank you all for coming today. I really didn't expect such a big crowd." Ashley scanned their faces, disappointed Vic wasn't among them.

She wasn't sure why she'd expected her to show up. Whatever they could have been was over now, a shriveled corpse in the realms of revenge.

Ashley had found a way to live with the closure. Though Vic lived inside the pages of every book she plotted and wrote.

As long as she held those images close to her heart, webbing through her mind, she was positive she'd be okay and that every day would be a new adventure, even if only on her monitor. Eventually, the pain of their separation would subside, and maybe then, just maybe, she'd move on to another rung of life. Maybe find a girlfriend she'd want to share her life with forever. She was no longer spitting in the face of love. She'd proved that it lived beyond the monitor and keyboard and never again would she believe it wasn't real. Without a doubt, she knew that simple four-letter word held one hell of a punch. And one day, she'd feel its binding strength again.

Ashley sat on the edge of the card table. Today she wore jeans, a tight red T-shirt tucked into the waistband, cut just low enough to show off her cleavage, and a new pair of black spiked boots which she felt so damn sexy wearing. No more boring business slacks or those binding silk blouses. Those were for her clients, not the hopeful faces of her erotic readers.

In this new world, she felt sexy outside the pages, where she was an erotic author, and she was going to dress for the occasion daily. Maybe Vic had something to do with the transformation, or maybe transforming herself with a keyboard was the answer. Either way, she loved her fresh, hip look and wanted to keep it.

"Read one of the sex scenes!" someone in the crowd shouted, snapping Ashley from her personal thoughts.

Ashley looked at the woman waving her book, her transparent blue eyes bright against her fluorescent red nose. "You want me to give away free sex?" She gave the woman her best cute smile.

The woman nodded and clapped, which goosed the rest into following. Before Ashley knew it, the whole room was rooting her on.

She flipped to one of the sections of the book with an edge folded in. She always kept a sex scene bookmarked. It was her favorite part, after all. "I won't give you free sex, but I'll sure take you right up to that wicked hot edge."

The crowd hooted as she opened the book. She couldn't resist a quick scan back over the women. She stalled on the spot where Vic had leaned against the wall the first time she ever laid eyes on her.

God how she wished she were standing there right now.

"In case any of you haven't read the book yet, Sellers fucked Tasha's girlfriend of six years. Tasha absolutely hates Sellers, of course, with good reason. They're now on a road trip across the map for reasons you'll have to find out for yourself when you buy the book." She looked over their faces with a smile. "But to cut a long story short, they've wound up in a hotel room in the middle of bum-fuck Texas, and I'll begin there."

She looked at the page and gave her fans what they wanted. Sex. And not behind closed doors. Or as close as she could get without giving away too much freebie sex.

Tipsy, Tasha unlocked the hotel door and stumbled through the doorway. To her shock, Sellers lay sprawled across the bed in nothing more than a pair of black boxers and a white T-shirt.

Her tanned legs were like smoke signals, begging Tasha to feel them, to taste them, to be wrapped between them.

Ashley stalled to let the rushed murmurs rumble over the audience. She already had their undivided attention, and their faces, so watchful, proved that.

Movement caught her eye and she looked in its direction. The owner sat in a chair and waved her to continue.

Why in hell was she still praying Vic would show up? This wasn't a fairy tale, and Vic wasn't going to swoop down like a butch archangel to save her. She didn't need saving anymore. She just needed love. Not just any love; she desperately wanted Vic's love.

She gave Linda a grin and looked back down.

With a grunt, Tasha collapsed in the chair and kicked off her high-heeled boots. "I thought you were taking that little twat back to her room to fuck like rabbits." Tasha almost cringed with the echo of jealousy ringing back on her ears.

Fuck if she didn't sound like a scorned lover. Okay, so she was a scorned lover, but not with this girlfriend-snatching bitch.

"Nah. She was too easy." Sellers shrugged and rolled onto her stomach to face the TV.

"Hasn't seemed to stop you from fucking anything else that stands still long enough," Tasha spat.

Sellers sat up in the center of the bed. "Are you more upset with me for fucking Hanna, or at Hanna for wanting to fuck me?"

Her question stunned Tasha. She'd never stopped her hatred toward Sellers long enough to point fingers at Hanna. Wasn't that where the blame should be? Hanna was supposed to be in love with her. She should have warded off any sexual advances from people like Sellers. Hell, from anyone for that matter.

Someone snorted and Ashley smiled. The lesbian world was a small one. Usually, when one woman dropped her girlfriend, someone close to her, in some horrible cases a best friend, was there to sweep her off her feet. That was, until the next piece of ass came along, which wasn't too long.

Ashley found her mark and started again.

Yet, obviously, she hadn't.

"Has it ever occurred to you that taken women are off limits?" Tasha ground her teeth and glared, shoving Hanna's blame away since Sellers was here to take her tongue-lashing.

"Has it ever occurred to you that taken women shouldn't be out fucking unattached women?" Sellers scooted toward the edge of the bed, her small breasts pushing against the fabric of her way too thin cotton T-shirt.

Tasha swallowed. She couldn't draw her gaze away from Sellers's nipples. They hypnotized her, so tantalizing and stiff. She wanted to lick them and then curl her tongue around their hardness.

"You should have enough courtesy to tell them no."

"They should have enough courtesy to never ask."

Tasha shoved out of the chair. This argument wasn't going anywhere and she needed a fucking cold shower to help clear her muddled mind. As soon as she rounded the edge of the bed, Sellers grabbed her wrist and spun her around.

Ashley looked out over their fixated gazes. Right now, she had them hook, line, and sinker. Sex sold. That proof was staring back at her from almost every face in the crowd.

She dared a glance back to that darkened spot against the far wall and her breath caught. Vic was there, watching her.

Something hot streaked across the opening of her pussy while her heart skipped way too many beats. God, would it always be this way if she ran into Vic? Would she always want her with such brutality?

Vic gave a single nod and Ashley returned the gesture with a smile. She wasn't sure what to make of Vic's presence. Hopefully she'd soon find out. But right now, she had a room full of readers who were waiting with bated breath for her to continue. And now she had someone who was fully dressed and sexy as fucking sin to read to.

She fixed her gaze on those penetrating eyes and read, once again, from memory.

> *Pain bit into her flesh as Sellers tugged her face-down onto the bed. She straddled Tasha's back and pinned her arms by her side.*
>
> *Tasha bucked, which only made Sellers tighten those lean legs even tighter.*
>
> *With her face nuzzled against Tasha's ear, her voice dipped into a "fuck me" growl. "You wanted to be the one to fuck me, didn't you?"*
>
> *"Get off me!" Tasha wiggled and tugged against the hands binding her.*
>
> *Sellers licked the edge of her ear then sucked the lobe between her teeth. "You could have forgiven her for fucking anyone but me, couldn't you?" She kneed Tasha's legs apart then ground against her ass. "You couldn't stand the thought of her making your dream reality. Isn't that right, sweet cheeks?"*

Vic's eyes never left her. They bored right into her soul. Ashley wanted her so bad it was caustic.

Tasha went limp against the mattress, woozy from the shots of liquor and crazy from need. She whimpered with heated anticipation and her pussy throbbed.

Dammit, Sellers was right. She'd wanted to fuck her. The thought of Hanna kissing those inviting lips, or fucking that fit body, filled her with more anger than the act itself.

Sellers ground her hips in lazy circles, driving Tasha over the brink of self-control. She let loose a soft cry and arched her back in submission.

The bitch ripped away her self-control one thrust at a time, one raspy-breathed word at a time. She had to rein her power back in.

The lie formed in her mind long before she heard it roll from her lips. "Just thinking about her hands on your well-used pussy made me want to throw up."

The maddening thrusts against her ass came to a brutal halt. Tasha instantly wanted to retract her words, wanted to recall each one, wanted Sellers to fuck her until nothing but her name gasped from her mouth.

"Liar." The urgent whisper against her ear sent a trail of fire through Tasha's pussy. Sellers pumped against her again, hard and deliberate, jolting Tasha against the mattress. "Would you like me to show you how I fucked her?" She shoved against Tasha again. "How I made her pant my name while I wrenched an orgasm from her body?" Once again, her hips slammed against Tasha.

A sharp whimper escaped before Tasha could snare the sound.

"How I fingered every hole in her body and listened to her scream for God?"

Ashley sucked back a whimper as images violated her mind—of Vic entering her, thrusting and stretching, sending her spiraling into the most erotic abyss she'd ever encountered. Her crotch seethed with fire, her mind so full it pounded.

She licked her lips and read.

With a sick knot forming in the pit of her stomach, Tasha nodded. As sick as the admission was, she wanted Sellers inside her, stealing her orgasm.

"Too bad." Sellers rolled off her, slammed into a pair of jeans, and grabbed her leather jacket. She towered at the end of the bed, her breathing haggard and eyes savagely hungry. "I'm not in the mood to give you the satisfaction."

Sellers spun around and barreled from the room. The hotel door slammed with a deafening whip crack.

Horny and defeated, Tasha slammed her forehead against the mattress several times. "Me and my fucking mouth!"

Ashley dragged her gaze away from Vic and laid the book down. The crowd grumbled with good sportsmanship, teasingly booing her for cutting off a sex scene, then they began clapping.

She smiled and gave a little curtsey. Her pride swelled, her ego thrilled, when she looked back out over them to find everyone completely dressed, the red noses gone from their faces, and all hair intact.

Maybe one day she could stand before a crowd without transforming them.

When she looked back to the darkened corner, Vic was still staring at her.

A strong current arced between them. No matter how many days, weeks, or years passed them by, no matter what sick games they'd played, and no matter who came out the winner or the loser, they would always have their precious time together to remember forever. All beginning with this very bookstore.

Linda approached and Ashley tore away from those fuck-me eyes.

"We have a few minutes for questions before we start lining up for the signing. I'd like everyone to start against the left wall to make an easier passage for those still shopping." She grinned. "Buy up, ladies."

With a wink, she walked away and Ashley braced herself for the questions. This part wasn't much easier than reading, but was tolerable.

"What's the name of your next release and when will it be on the market?" a woman in the front row who held hands with her partner asked.

"*Forever Kiss* comes out at the end of the year. After that is *Sweet Seduction*." Ashley forced herself not to look at Vic.

"Are you going to the Saints and Sinners convention next year?" A butch in the back row stood up.

"I plan to attend since I'll have another release in that month. Besides, I need more visuals for my next work in progress." Ashley shrugged. "I have to admit I've never been too far outside Arizona's door."

The woman sat back down.

"Will you be on one of the panels?" another woman on the end of the middle row asked.

"Heavens above, hell no! It's all I can manage just to read a few pages in front of you guys. I'd keel over before I could give the first word of any speech."

The woman chuckled and blurted out another question. "Could you ever see yourself writing regular romance without sex?"

Ashley slowly shook her head. The door for romance had slammed shut firmly behind her. Without a doubt, she knew she'd never write sex behind closed doors again. "Would you want me to?"

"Fuck no!"

Once again, the crowd broke into laughter while Linda came to stand beside the card table. Just as she opened her mouth, no doubt to urge on the signing, another question came from the crowd.

"Are you single?" the same woman who'd inquired about the next book asked. Her partner playfully goosed her and everyone snickered.

Ashley automatically looked at Vic. That penetrating stare still locked on her turned her insides into a battle zone.

"Yes, as a matter of fact, I'm single." Ashley looked back at the woman. "Sorry, my threesome story hasn't been written yet." She winked at the woman's partner.

The crowd roared. After several minutes, they hushed and Ashley looked out over them, waiting for the next question.

"Have you ever written from first-hand experience?"

Ashley would know that voice anywhere. The sound climbed over her body in reckless waves of smoldering heat. Her crotch throbbed as she looked at Vic.

God, had she ever written from first-hand experience. "As a matter of fact, I have. Nothing wrong with a little hands-on research to add to the yummy flavor of a sex scene." Ashley held her head a bit higher as the audience snickered. She wasn't ashamed anymore. Caprice was right. There was always a little truth in every book and any author who said different was lying through their teeth. "You of all people should know that, Vic."

Hushed murmurs wove through the rows of chairs. The women turned as one to look at Vic, straining to get a clear view of her. Some smiled and jostled each other when they recognized the name from the dedication. Others gave her a hard stare as if they were assessing her sexual prowess, or wondering just how close her relationship to Ashley was and trying to decide how much of the story centered on personal experience.

All heads turned back to Ashley, seeking confirmation of their assumptions.

Ashley held tight to the smile on her face. It took every ounce of willpower she possessed not to push away from the table, fly across the room, and crash into Vic with the force of a free-rolling locomotive.

When the silence became too unbearable, not to mention Vic's smoldering stare, Ashley stood. "I've exercised these fingers all day. What say we sign some books?"

Women laughed and Ashley realized what she'd said and held

up her hand to wiggle her fingers, which only spurred the women into hysterics.

When Ashley glanced back to the far wall, Vic was nowhere in sight. Her heart sank. After getting in her barb about first-hand experience, Vic hadn't waited around to speak to her or watch her sign the books.

Had Vic gotten the confession she wanted? Hadn't the dedication in *Phantom* proved Ashley wasn't above giving credit where credit was due? Was her presence here today an indication that she'd forgiven Ashley?

With a smile, she decided the latter was the answer, or rather it was the answer she was going to believe. She'd just admitted in front of an entire audience that Vic meant something to her. It had better be good enough.

With her head held high and her spirits peaked, Ashley dove into her new life. She was a published author now, had reached her dream, and she'd be damned if anything got in the way of that happiness. She deserved every ounce of this thrill. And her supporters deserved her undivided attention.

Book after book, she signed her name. She couldn't think of another feeling greater than the one coursing through her now. And just when she thought her wrist would give out, she looked up to find the last female in line—the very one who asked about her attendance at next year's book convention and stood out in the crowd with her skate-boarder look.

Her hands stuffed into her pockets, *Phantom* tucked under her arm, she smiled. "I really enjoyed both of your books and can't wait to read the next in line."

"Thank you. I really enjoyed writing them."

As if she suddenly remembered what she was doing, the woman yanked her hand from her pocket and handed Ashley the book. "Can you sign this to Patty?"

Ashley opened to the first page. "Patty. You don't strike me as a Patty for some reason." She wouldn't dare admit the woman looked more like a Patrick than a Patty. Dressed in jeans drooping over a pair of plaid boxers, a canary yellow golf shirt with the collar pulled up into a stiff peak, the woman screamed youth.

A smile swept across her face. The sweet expression warmed Ashley. "Patty is my girlfriend. She wants to be a writer."

"That's great. Tell her to keep at it and never give up on her dream. There's no other feeling in the world like holding your first book in your hands, or the second."

Ashley handed the book back and the woman gave a firm nod. "I'll tell her you said that."

She watched as the woman walked toward the exit and remembered those first twitches of characters dancing in her mind, how they'd consumed her, scratching and clawing, until she finally unleashed their story. Of course, that first novel wasn't the first released, but still, that feeling was just as fresh now as it had been all those years ago.

"Hey!" Ashley called out to her.

The woman turned around and raised an eyebrow in question.

"Tell her to e-mail me. I have the best beta reader in the world. She'd be thrilled to give her some advice." Ashley was sure she'd never hear the end of Caprice scolding her for volunteering her services, but last Ashley checked, Caprice owed her one. She'd never gotten her lap dance from Dan.

The woman's face lit up with her smile. "You're awesome! I'll tell her. She'll be spazzed."

Long after the crowd had vanished, Ashley folded the legs of the card table and leaned it against the back wall. "Well, that went well."

Linda dropped a box onto the floor in front of a bookshelf. "Your fan club will continue to grow and I truly appreciate you bringing the business my way."

"No, thank you for supporting me the way you have. We're a small world. We need all the help we can get."

With a final hug, Ashley took her copy of *Phantom* and made her way into the bright sunshine. Heat pricked her skin as she pulled her sunglasses into place and started down the sidewalk toward her car.

She froze and her gut clamped tight when she found Vic leaned casually against the brick facing of the storefront, one foot cocked back and resting against the wall.

Vic turned her way and a smile stretched those sweet lips. "Hi, sexy."

Ashley hugged the book to her stomach, afraid the butterflies would take flight. "Hi there, yourself."

"Did you miss me?"

"No. Why would I?" Ashley teased and took several steps toward her, dangerously close.

"Because no one gives you plotlines like these hands can." Vic grabbed her wrist and pulled her into the alcove between the stores. She wedged Ashley against the brick and clamped their mouths together. Her tongue forced inside and curled around Ashley's.

Heaven. She was heaven.

When she pulled back, Ashley almost spilled to the concrete, her legs like cotton wool from the adrenaline rush.

Vic stared down over her. "I need you."

Ashley bit back a relieved sigh. "Good. I need you to need me."

"I want you."

"Even better. Want keeps you needing."

Vic pressed her forehead against Ashley's. "I love you."

Ashley draped her arms around her neck. "I know."

Vic chuckled as she pulled Ashley tighter against her body. "You do, huh?"

Ashley nodded. "You love me because you're afraid I'll make you some ugly hag in my next novel. Or worse, the janitor or bus boy in a five-star restaurant named Ellirondos."

Vic laughed and pressed her lips against Ashley's. "God forbid."

Ashley kissed her, long and lingering, her heart overflowing its boundaries. When she pulled back, she knew she had Vic forever. "Now, I need you to take me home. I have some hands-on research to experience…on a staircase. Again."

"With pleasure. Besides, I need your autograph. Again."

About the Author

Larkin Rose lives in a "blink and you've missed it" town in the beautiful state of South Carolina with her partner, Rose (hence the pen name), a portion of their seven brats, two chunky grandsons, and too many animals to name. Her writing career began four years ago when the voices in her head wouldn't stop their constant chatter. After ruling out multiple personalities and hitting the keyboard, a writer was born.

Larkin's work can also be found in *Ultimate Lesbian Erotica 2008* and *Wetter 2008* (both writing as Sheri Livingston).

The voices continue. The clatter of keys continues. The birth of erotic creations carries on.

Books Available From Bold Strokes Books

Witch Wolf by Winter Pennington. In a world where vampires have charmed their way into modern society, where werewolves walk the streets with their beasts disguised by human skin, Investigator Kassandra Lyall has a secret of her own to protect. She's one of them. (978-1-60282-177-4)

Do Not Disturb by Carsen Taite. Ainsley Faraday, a high-powered executive, and rock music celebrity Greer Davis couldn't be less well suited for one another, and yet they soon discover passion has a way of designing its own future. (978-1-60282-153-8)

From This Moment On by PJ Trebelhorn. Devon Conway and Katherine Hunter both lost love and neither believes they will ever find it again—until the moment they meet and everything changes. (978-1-60282-154-5)

Vapor by Larkin Rose. When erotic romance writer Ashley Vaughn decides to take her research into the bedroom for a night of passion with Victoria Hadley, she discovers that fact is hotter than fiction. (978-1-60282-155-2)

Wind and Bones by Kristin Marra. Jill O'Hara, award-winning journalist, just wants to settle her deceased father's affairs and leave Prairie View, Montana, far, far behind—but an old girlfriend, a sexy sheriff, and a dangerous secret keep her down on the ranch. (978-1-60282-150-7)

Nightshade by Shea Godfrey. The story of a princess, betrothed as a political pawn, who falls for her intended husband's soldier sister, is a modern-day fairy tale to capture the heart. (978-1-60282-151-4)

Vieux Carré Voodoo by Greg Herren. Popular New Orleans detective Scotty Bradley just can't stay out of trouble—especially when an old flame turns up asking for help. (978-1-60282-152-1)

The Pleasure Set by Lisa Girolami. Laney DeGraff, a successful president of a family-owned bank on Rodeo Drive, finds her comfortable life taking a turn toward danger when Theresa Aguilar, a sleek, sexy lawyer, invites her to join an exclusive, secret group of powerful, alluring women. (978-1-60282-144-6)

A Perfect Match by Erin Dutton. The exciting world of pro golf forms the backdrop for a fast-paced, sexy romance. (978-1-60282-145-3)

Father Knows Best by Lynda Sandoval. High school juniors and best friends Lila Moreno, Meryl Morganstern, and Caressa Thibodoux plan to make the most of the summer before senior year. What they discover that amazing summer about girl power, growing up, and trusting friends and family more than prepares them to tackle that all-important senior year! (978-1-60282-147-7)

The Midnight Hunt by L.L. Raand. Medic Drake McKennan takes a chance and loses, and her life will never be the same—because when she wakes up after surviving a life-threatening illness, she is no longer human. (978-1-60282-140-8)

Long Shot by D. Jackson Leigh. Love isn't safe, which is exactly why equine veterinarian Tory Greyson wants no part of it—until Leah Montgomery and a horse that won't give up convince her otherwise. (978-1-60282-141-5)

In Medias Res by Yolanda Wallace. Sydney has forgotten her entire life, and the one woman who holds the key to her memory, and her heart, doesn't want to be found. (978-1-60282-142-2)

Awakening to Sunlight by Lindsey Stone. Neither Judith or Lizzy is looking for companionship, and certainly not love—but when their lives become entangled, they discover both. (978-1-60282-143-9)

Fever by VK Powell. Hired gun Zakaria Chambers is hired to provide a simple escort service to philanthropist Sara Ambrosini, but nothing is as simple as it seems, especially love. (978-1-60282-135-4)

Truths by Rebecca S. Buck. Two women separated by two hundred years are connected by fate and love. (978-1-60282-146-0)

High Risk by JLee Meyer. Can actress Kate Hoffman really risk all she's worked for to take a chance on love? Or is it already too late? (978-1-60282-136-1)

Missing Lynx by Kim Baldwin and Xenia Alexiou. On the trail of a notorious serial killer, Elite Operative Lynx's growing attraction to a mysterious mercenary could be her path to love—or to death. (978-1-60282-137-8)

Spanking New by Clifford Henderson. A poignant, hilarious, unforgettable look at life, love, gender, and the essence of what makes us who we are. (978-1-60282-138-5)

Magic of the Heart by C.J. Harte. CEO Susan Hettinger and wild, impulsive rock star M.J. Carson couldn't be more different if they tried—but opposites attract in ways neither woman can resist. (978-1-60282-131-6)

Ambereye by Gill McKnight. Jolie Garoul is falling in love with her assistant. The big problem is, Jolie is a werewolf. (978-1-60282-132-3)

Collision Course by C.P. Rowlands. Tragedy leaves Brie O'Malley and Jordan Carter fearful and alone. Can they find the courage to take a second chance on love? (978-1-60282-133-0)

Mephisto Aria by Justine Saracen. Opera singer Katherina Marov's destiny may be to repeat the mistakes of her father when she becomes involved in a dangerous love affair. (978-1-60282-134-7)

Battle Scars by Meghan O'Brien. Returning Iraq war veteran Ray McKenna struggles with the battle scars that can only be healed by love. (978-1-60282-129-3)

Chaps by Jove Belle. Eden Metcalf wants nothing more than to flee from her troubled past and travel the open road—until she runs into rancher Brandi Cornwell. (978-1-60282-127-9)

Lightbearer by John Caruso. Lucifer dares to question the premise of creation itself and reveals that sin may be all that stands between us and living hell. (978-1-60282-130-9)

The Seeker by Ronica Black. FBI profiler Kennedy Scott battles ghosts from her past, deadly obsession, and the evil that haunts her. (978-1-60282-128-6)

Power Play by Julie Cannon. Businesswomen Tate Monroe and Victoria Sosa are at odds in the boardroom, but not in the bedroom. (978-1-60282-125-5)

The Remarkable Journey of Miss Tranby Quirke by Elizabeth Ridley. When love enters Tranby's life in the form of a beautiful nineteen-year-old student, Lysette McDonald, she embarks on the most remarkable journey of all. (978-1-60282-126-2)

Returning Tides by Radclyffe. Insurance investigator Ashley Walker faces more than a dangerous opponent when she returns to the town, and the woman, she left behind. (978-1-60282-123-1)

Veritas by Anne Laughlin. When the hallowed halls of academia become the stage for murder, newly appointed Dean Beth Ellis's search for the truth leads her to unexpected discoveries about her own heart. (978-1-60282-124-8)

The Pleasure Planner by Larkin Rose. Pleasure purveyor Bree Hendricks treats love like a commodity until Logan Delaney makes Bree the client in her own game. (978-1-60282-121-7)

everafter by Nell Stark and Trinity Tam. Valentine Darrow is bitten by a vampire on her way to propose to her lover Alexa Newland, and their lives and love are placed in mortal jeopardy. (978-1-60282-119-4)

Beggar of Love by Lee Lynch. Jefferson is the lover every woman wants to be—or to have. A revealing saga of lesbian sexuality. (978-1-60282-122-4)